CHOOSING YOU

LENA HENDRIX

To bad boys everywhere—watch out. The good girls are coming for you.

ABOUT THIS BOOK

I'm the new girl in town. The oldest daughter of an affluent banker. *Old money.*

He's a lost soul from the wrong side of the tracks—and he has a reputation. Everyone knows to stay away from sinfully gorgeous mechanic Matthew Bailey.

When our paths cross and he offers me a smirk and a ride on his motorcycle, I try to refuse, but he's too tempting to resist. Sneaking off with the town bad boy will help me break free of my family's stifling expectations.

But being with Matthew puts everything at stake—my reputation, my family, my heart.

Every look, every touch, is electric. Our sizzling summer romance is flirting dangerously toward a deeper connection—one that will upturn both our lives.

Matthew is used to being alone. Abandoned. Now it's up to me to show him what it means to be the one worth choosing.

READER NOTE

This book contains adult material including references to alcohol abuse and child neglect.

It is my hope that I've handled these topics with the care and research they deserve.

ONE
CHARLOTTE

My mother was porcelain, flawless in every sense, and any tiny cracks that dared appear were expertly concealed. This included cracks in her face as well as in her family.

I sat next to her at Francesca's Italian restaurant in Chikalu Falls, Montana, feeling not only like a crack, but a chasm. I smoothed my hands down the silk fabric of my skirt and calmed my face. I hated this town. I missed St. Louis.

My plastic smile remained in place as we exchanged polite conversation with the family of my father's business associate. The couple sat directly across from us, my father rubbing elbows with the businessman. My little sister, Amber, sat to my left. She was only sixteen and perfectly content to enjoy a life of fancy dresses and expensive dinners.

"Charlotte, how do you like Chikalu Falls so far, dear?" Mrs. Hutchins smiled at me. Her soft brown curls, expertly styled. Her red lips perfectly painted despite the heaping swirls of spaghetti she shoveled into her face.

I swallowed past the lie that hung in my throat. "It's

lovely." My mother regarded me but gave a slight nod of approval.

I let the din of conversation flow over me as I looked around the small restaurant. From what I could tell, Francesca's was the nicest eatery in the entire town. Couples dotted the main floor, some wearing slacks and dresses, others jeans and T-shirts. It was everything a stereotypical Italian American restaurant should be. Bold, rich colors, candles, cheap wine, hearty portions.

I pushed the linguini and clams around my plate. The food was exceptional, I'd give Francesca that. Had my stomach not been in knots the entire evening, I would have loved to dive into it with as much gusto as Mrs. Hutchins.

Amber kicked my foot under the table. I shot her a glare, my lips in a firm line. Glancing around, she stuck the tip of her tongue out at me. Slyly looking over, I crossed my eyes in her direction. A bubble of laughter burst out of her. I bit the inside of my lip as Mother's tone turned to ice. "Ladies. Behave yourselves."

"Yes, ma'am," we said in unison. I reached under the table to playfully pinch the outside of Amber's thigh and give her a wink.

The Good-Time Assassin is back with a vengeance.

Had Mother known that was our nickname for her, she'd be horrified. In her world, women were to be calm, put together. Know their place.

Dinner slogged on. I couldn't have cared less for the conversations over financial planning, bills, and Montana billionaires. Despite being only twenty-two, my father was entrusting me to open a new Montana branch of Perry Investments. I should have been engaging in meaningful conversation. Instead, I made note of the wildly eclectic makeup of the residents of Chikalu Falls.

Our social circle in St. Louis had been small—only the elite, private school types had surrounded us. Here, it felt like the Wild West.

I also let my mind wander to earlier this afternoon. Daddy had purchased a small home on the outskirts of town as yet another "investment opportunity" and it would be mine to live in while I got the branch up and running. My family would not be staying once I was settled. I would be left to prove my mettle.

After hours of cleaning and rearranging until Mother felt the house was perfect, I'd stepped outside to catch my breath. It sat on a large corner lot, a few blocks from downtown.

Under the metal streetlamp was a small bench, and Mother had noted that the landscapers would be removing it when they cleared the other gardens. We'd been forbidden from sitting at it so the neighbors wouldn't think we were "trollops" posted on the corner. She always did have a flair for the dramatic.

Relaxing on the bench, I looked out onto my new neighborhood. Warm May air carried the pine and earthy smell of the Montana mountains. The roar of an engine ripped through the quiet, and I glanced up the street to see a thundering motorcycle speeding down the road. As it approached, time slowed. Straddling the motorcycle was a strikingly handsome man. My breath caught as his long, thick legs stretched the denim of his jeans. Corded arms flexed as the rumbling machine drew closer. I couldn't see his eyes behind the mirrored sunglasses, but his head slanted toward me.

As quickly as he'd approached, he was gone.

Who the hell had that been?

Moments later, the motorcycle came back down the

road in the opposite direction. My heart hammered against my ribs as he slowed to a halt in front of me. I looked around, certain he wasn't stopping to talk to me.

I watched a thick vein rope up his forearm as he swung a long leg over his bike. The stranger sauntered toward me, and I stared at him, unabashedly appreciating the cut lines of his muscular frame.

I pressed my thighs together, a hot jolt of electricity igniting my insides.

"You're new." The stranger's voice was gravel over velvet, strong and deep.

I lifted my chin and gave him a small smile. "I am."

The man crossed his arms just as the screen door slammed and my sister came running out of the house, breaking the spell. "Mother needs you!"

I stood, hating to walk away without talking to him more, having a proper introduction, but I knew I had to leave before Mother came looking for me herself. As I walked away, I looked back to find the man mounted on his motorcycle, tracking my movements back toward the house.

Holy hell he's hot.

My name being spoken at the table ripped me from the scandalous memory. "Charlotte is absolutely thrilled to be managing the new branch for Richard."

Thrilled.

When my father made the family decision to expand his financial planning and investment firm to Montana, we didn't dare question it. He claimed that Montana's recent influx of California millionaires, settling in bigger cities like Bozeman, were ripe for the picking. He'd been grooming me to take over the family business, so uprooting my comfortable life and transplanting me in Nowhere, Montana, had made perfect sense to him.

I didn't argue but did what was expected of me. *Again.*

My practiced, polite smile eased across my face without effort. It had become a part of me, just like the canned responses that accompanied any questions about our family.

"Charlotte will also be joining the local Women's Club."

Mrs. Hutchins clasped her hands in delight. "They'll be *tickled* to have you! Imagine someone with such a world-view bringing new ideas to Chikalu."

I wasn't sure St. Louis qualified as much of a worldview, and my mother despised the idea of my joining a local club chapter rather than the country club a few towns over. I fought tooth and nail and finally convinced her that my presence in the Women's Club could further the family name in our new town.

For me, it was an escape.

For an hour a week I could shed the poised, practiced demeanor of a *well-bred woman* and simply be Charlotte. Or, at least, begin to figure out who the hell Charlotte was supposed to be.

CRISP MAY AIR slowly surrendered to warm June breezes. I sucked in the fresh mountain air and let it ruffle the strands of my hair. The sun was shining, nothing but blue skies and wide-open spaces.

Montana has its perks.

After a long day staring at pages and pages of numbers and receipts with nothing but stale office air and burned coffee, I was eager to soak up the late-afternoon sun. Instead of heading toward my parents' house, I used my membership in the Women's Club as an excuse to stay downtown.

The Friday meetings for the Chikalu Women's Club had become the highlight of my week. Despite my initial reservations, the women who served in the club were a delight.

With a healthy mix of generations, the Women's Club maintained a primary focus on community outreach and philanthropy. Behind closed doors, they also served up wine and gossip like nobody's business.

On the bench, I tipped my face toward the sun.

"Ugh. Stop being so pretty." Disgust dripped from Trina's voice as she approached behind me. My smile, my *real* smile, cracked my face wide open.

I had met Trina through the Women's Club. She was around my age, and despite my reserved exterior at our first meeting, she had sidled up next to me and determined that we'd be fast friends.

My hand shielded the slanting rays of the sun. "Just trying to keep up with you."

Trina rolled her eyes and smiled before plopping beside me on the bench. Trina was free in all the best ways. Her tawny brown hair curled wildly around her shoulders. Her eyes were lined in a bright aqua blue. Trina always had mischief in her eyes and a smile on her lips. As far as I could tell, she had an endless supply of happiness. It was hard to be grumpy around someone like that.

"Do you want to go out tonight?"

My parents and sister weren't leaving for Missouri for another week or so, and I considered my evening routine of small talk with them followed by pinochle or reading in the den.

Snoozefest.

"I could go out. What did you have in mind?"

"I honestly don't care, as long as it involves some bad

decisions." Her grin curled up at the edges, and one dimple deepened on her cheek.

I bumped her shoulder with mine. "Slow down, wildcat."

"Come on. One night. Let your hair down." She reached over to my cardigan, buttoned to the top. "Loosen up a little."

I shrugged her off. "Leave me alone. I am loose."

At the subtle innuendo, we both burst out laughing.

Trina tucked a runaway curl behind her ear. "I know there's a freak beneath all those sweater sets. Just be *you*."

Her words hit an unexpected nerve. I would be me, if I had a fucking clue who me was.

But in the four weeks I'd known her, Trina sparked something inside me, a small ember that burned to figure out exactly what I wanted. Who I was. I had never allowed myself to explore my true self. Every decision was carefully crafted and my parents' opinions heavily weighed.

At twenty-two, I was already exhausted. I was also secretly thrilled at the prospect of running into the handsome stranger on the motorcycle. I hadn't seen him at all in this small town and was starting to think I'd invented him.

"Fine," I conceded.

"Yes!" Trina's arms shot straight above her head. "We are getting you laid."

I laughed with her. "Slow down. I said I'd go out tonight for a few drinks. Getting laid is not on the docket."

"We'll see about that." Trina wiggled her eyebrows, then stuck one finger in the air as a thought came to her. "But I get to dress you."

TWO
MATTHEW

THE HUM in my veins was developing into a slow ache. I couldn't relax. The old floor in my shitty apartment above the mechanic's garage where I worked creaked under my boots as I wore a path between the door and window. Adrenaline coursed through me as my heart beat against my rib cage. I balled my hand into a fist, the pain radiating up my arm.

I wanted to hit something. *Again.*

What had started off as a quick run to the store had ruined my entire goddamn day. Outside of Richardson's grocery store, I stumbled on my little brother, Kevin. Still in high school, Kevin was living with my father. It had been years since our mother had died, and without her, no one but me was looking out for him. Kevin was gaunt and slimmer since I'd last seen him.

"Hi, Matty." He could barely look me in the eyes.

"What are you doing here? I thought you were taking that extra summer class? Isn't there school today?"

He smirked like it was a stupid thing for me to assume he'd be in class. Kevin was smart—brilliant, really—and despite his terrible attendance, he could ace any class he decided to show up for. He didn't have much else to say, but when he turned to leave, I saw the fresh bruise blooming just under his short-sleeve shirt.

"The fuck is that?" I gestured toward his arm. "He do that to you?"

Kevin's face went tight and his jaw flexed. I knew the truth. My father's drinking had steadily increased in our mother's absence, and whenever he felt the need, he used his own kids as a way to vent his sadness and the frustrations over the choices he'd made.

Kevin wouldn't talk about it. "Come on." I angled my head toward the store. Together we stocked up on snack bars and jerky and bottled water—all nonperishables because he'd be hiding them beneath his bed. My stomach churned at the thought.

"Stay with me. I've got a couch you could crash on."

He shook his head.

"Kevin, you can't live like this."

"It's not that bad. Most days are pretty good days." Defeat darkened his already pale features. "I can't give up on him."

Anger snaked itself up my back and around my throat. Our oldest brother, Danny, had left Chikalu as soon as he was able and never looked back. I stayed behind under the guise of helping Dad and Kevin. It had been years, and I'd done nothing but watch Kevin grow into a young man who bucked authority and sported new bruises he hid with hoodies and who wasn't living up to his potential. I wasn't helping anyone.

Before he left, I slipped a twenty into the pocket of his hoodie. "Just in case. And think about what I said."

Kevin nodded and slunk back toward the alley. "And hey," I added, "go to school on Monday."

I smiled and he smirked. My chest ached and my head throbbed.

Back in my apartment, I stopped pacing and leaned my forearms against the wall. My head hung low, and I steadied my breathing. There had to be something—anything—I could do to keep Kevin safe. Despite his spotty attendance, Kevin had good grades and at my insistence had applied to a few colleges and universities. I had no idea if he'd heard back from any yet. College may never have been in the cards for me, but for him it could be, and he deserved more than the local community college. He needed to get far away from here.

Escape.

The shrill ring of my phone had me pushing off the wall and padding toward the kitchen.

"Yeah."

"Mr. Bailey, Gregg Morgan."

Fuck.

"Yes, sir. What can I do for you?"

"I've been thinking about you since your visit to the recruitment office. Have you given any more thought to enlistment in the United States Marine Corps. The country could use a man like you in its ranks."

My chest pinched. I couldn't recall the last time someone had said anything even remotely positive about me, and it was uncomfortable to hear.

I cleared the lump from my throat. "I've given it some thought." The truth was, I thought about it every day. A chance to serve my country, work hard, and finally make something of myself. I hadn't wanted anything more.

"Housing, food, medical care, you wouldn't have to

worry about any of that. We can even get you set up with an education, son."

When I'd first spoken to the recruiter, I hadn't known that Dad's drinking had gotten worse, or that Kevin was taking the brunt of his frustrations and skipping school. There was no way I could pick up and leave him behind. My dream of serving my country would have to wait.

"Yeah, it's a good deal. There are a few things I'm hoping to get in order here first. I help my family out, and money is kind of an issue."

"Sure, sure, I recall us talking about that. It's good of you, son. I also had some ideas about that. Why don't you come down to the office and we can talk about it?"

I scrubbed my hand and squeezed the back of my neck. From what I could tell Gregg Morgan was a decent guy, and he understood my desire to serve as a Marine. What he didn't know was that since my first visit to the enlistment office, my life had gone completely off the rails. "Sure. Fine."

We agreed on a date and time to meet. I knew I couldn't commit in the way I so desperately wanted to, but I could at least hear the man out.

THREE
CHARLOTTE

"I REALLY FEEL like there was a bit more to this dress when we left." I tugged at the short hemline and prayed no one would report back to Mother and Daddy that they had seen me out with so little clothing.

Trina swatted my hand. "Don't you dare. It's Friday night, we're out, and you look amazing."

I flattened my hand against my stomach, willing the butterflies to settle. The flowing material of the dress accentuated my curves in ways I hadn't ever dared to show off. Though the dress was several inches shorter than I was used to, it fit perfectly. I felt trendy and electrified to be somewhere so far out of my comfort zone.

The Dirty Pigeon was just that—filthy. I peeled each shoe off the floor with a stomach-churning slurping sound as we waited to be served. Trina pressed her chest to the marred wood of the bar top as she leaned forward, trying to get the attention of the bartender on the opposite side. The crowd didn't seem to mind the dim lighting and sticky floors. It was a rowdy mix of happy faces—ones I was finally beginning to recognize from the firm or from walking downtown—and the tired, worn looks of those who were glad to be done with a long week of work.

A jukebox stood sentry at the center of the back wall, country music pumping out of its speakers. I scanned the crowd again, hope creeping up my throat as I searched for the handsome stranger.

"Here." Trina set a small shot glass in front of me as the bartender slid a beer behind it. "Shoot that and sip this."

My eyes went wide at the dark liquid. "What is it?"

Trina grinned. "Does it matter?"

Not wanting to disappoint my only friend, I lifted the shot glass to my nose. It burned in a way only hard alcohol could. My lips pressed themselves together as I swallowed hard. I would just have to power through and get it over with.

"Bottoms up." Before I could change my mind, I flipped my wrist, tipping the shot into my mouth. I held my breath to fight the urge to cough and make a fool of myself in front of Trina. Her head whipped back, her shot going down smoothly. A small cough escaped my burning throat.

"Chase it." Trina pushed the beer to my mouth, and I attempted a sip around another cough.

"Sorry," I squeaked.

"You don't have to apologize to me. You'll get the hang of it. Now let's find a table and some boys to dance!"

With a twirl, Trina moved away from the bar and into the center of the open space. A small clearing in the center of the bar served as a dance floor, with several small high-top tables littering the edges. Trina found an open table and perched on the stool to look around.

Chikalu Falls had a community college, and a table or two had groups of younger people. The rule-following part of me wondered silently if anyone was checking their IDs.

Beer wasn't my favorite, but after a few small sips, I could feel my shoulders relax. At the very least, the people-watching alone was entertaining.

Trina seemed to know everyone in town. If they didn't stop by the table, she'd wave eagerly across the dance floor.

"Are you ready to shake what your mama gave you?"

"Trust me, my mama wouldn't *dare*."

Trina grinned and clinked her beer bottle to mine. "Well, here's to women who aren't afraid to take up space." She grabbed my wrist and gently pulled me to the dance floor.

My face burned with embarrassment. My movements felt choppy and off beat, but soon I closed my eyes, and the low bass of the music swept me away. Trina danced with wild abandon, and her enthusiasm was infectious. As the dance floor filled in, we moved with the music, sang the lyrics off-key and too loudly, and laughed our way through the songs we didn't know.

Out of breath, I left Trina on the dance floor to get us another round. As I walked toward the back of the bar, my steps faltered. Sitting on a stool, looking hot as hell, was *him*. Friends and conversation all around him, he sat, shoulders hunched and a glass of clear liquid in his hand. His piercing green eyes tracked my movements. I was drawn to him, moving closer without breaking our eye contact.

He shifted on the stool to face me. A crisp white T-shirt stretched across his broad shoulders. The fabric strained against his biceps. The shirt was tucked into worn denim. His jeans were faded and had a spot or two—grease, maybe? —and his black motorcycle boots were scuffed.

If James Dean was six foot and built like a machine, this man would be a dead ringer.

I tamped down the nerves that fluttered in my belly as I boldly walked up to him. "Hey, stranger."

A smile played at his lips as he lifted the drink and took a sip. I watched his throat bob as he swallowed, and I caught myself swallowing hard right along with him.

"Evening, ma'am."

I tipped an eyebrow. "Ma'am? Really?"

He grinned—all bright-white teeth and a flash of charm.

My chest pinched. He was even more handsome when he smiled. I stuck out my hand. "I'm Charlotte."

He took my hand in his. His large palm was rough, and his long fingers wrapped around my hand. It was warm and subtly stained—the hands of a working man. He gave my hand a small squeeze, and electricity crackled up my arm. "Matthew."

"What can I get you?" the bartender said, cutting in and breaking the spell.

I blinked and held up my empty bottle. "Um, two more of these, please." I turned to Matthew. "What are you drinking? Can I buy you one?"

"No, ma'am. Just water for me, but even if it wasn't, that's not how it works around here."

I frowned as the bartender moved to grab the beers. "Not how what works?"

He laughed to himself and took another sip before reaching for his wallet and making eye contact with the bartender. "Those are on me."

Heat spread through me as his eyes traced back to me. I brushed a stray hair away from my face. "Thank you." I exhaled and looked around. "Here with friends?"

Someone to his left must have overheard, because a hand clamped down on his shoulder, and they shared a word and a laugh.

"Yeah. Just killing time. You?"

I angled my head toward Trina, who had stopped dancing to stare—her eyes wide and jaw slack. I shot her a silent, confused look—*What?*—before returning my attention to Matthew. "Yes. As you noticed, I'm new. My friend Trina is showing me around."

"Like what you see?" His eyes raked over my face, and I could feel prickly heat creep up my neck. Matthew smelled like leather and smoke and a little gasoline.

Strong. Manly. Intoxicating.

I set my beer down on the bar. I needed to slow down if my head felt like it was swimming because a man smelled like gasoline. I couldn't help it. He was so unlike any man I'd ever spoken with. The men I had briefly dated had all been boys from school or dates set up by my parents. Sons and nephews of their friends. Clean-shaven, *proper* boys.

There was nothing clean and proper about him, and that was not a boy in front of me. No, Matthew was definitely all man, a fact my body was acutely aware of.

"Chikalu Falls has been very nice."

Matthew laughed into his sip of water. My cheeks flamed in embarrassment, though I wasn't sure why. "There's a lot more to Chikalu than bake sales and weekly meetings. Certainly more than the Dirty Pidge."

Just then, Trina walked up and looped her arm with mine. "There you are!" Her cheeks were flushed, and she gently pulled me toward the dance floor. "You ready?"

I glanced at Matthew, and he swiveled back toward the bar.

"Um, sure." I reached a hand out and placed it on his arm. His steely eyes met mine and rooted me in place. "Maybe you can show me something new sometime."

His mouth tipped up in a smirk, and my heart flopped over.

"What are you doing?" Trina's voice was low but insistent. "Don't you know who that is?" She let out a breath. "Of course you don't. Sorry. Matthew Bailey is trouble. As in trouble with a capital T."

I sneaked a glance over my shoulder to see Matthew talking with a few of his friends. "He seems nice enough to me."

"He's not. His family is a disaster, and his dad is mean as a snake. Didn't you see his busted-up knuckles? He's a brawler. C'mon, let's go."

As we gathered our things, my eyes tracked down the lean, corded muscles of his forearm. Sure enough, red scrapes dragged across his knuckles. My teeth sank into my bottom lip. Trina knew more about the residents of Chikalu Falls, but there was something alluring about Matthew Bailey.

Dangerous, sure . . . but also delicious.

FOUR
MATTHEW

MAYBE YOU CAN SHOW me something new sometime.

The next afternoon, Charlotte's words clanged around in my skull. There was plenty I'd love to show her, and it didn't have fuck all to do with Chikalu. I could show her all kinds of dirty and devious things.

I wiped down the hood of the Chevelle and shook my head. Charlotte wasn't the kind of girl that would be down for quick and dirty, and there was something about her that made me feel wrong for even thinking about it. She was perfect—gorgeous and assertive and charming. She'd also been unafraid to talk to me, which was new and unexpected.

No, women like Charlotte didn't get down and dirty with men like me. They preferred the loafered, polo-wearing types I'd seen when I was hired to fix the golf carts at the country club.

Everything about her screamed demure and proper and *expensive*. Everything but that hot-as-fuck dress she wore. I'd bet my last paycheck her friend had talked her into wearing it. I'd owe Trina a drink if it weren't for her pulling

Charlotte away just as I was about to ask her to take a ride on my bike.

It was for the best, though. I had no right to assume Charlotte would dare go slumming with Bailey trash.

Goddamn could I show her a good time, though.

I checked the clock and cursed myself for getting lost in the engine rebuild. I slammed the hood down, stalked toward the sink, and did my best to scrub the grease from my hands with the industrial-strength orange hand cleaner. Streaks of black still stained my cuticles, but it would have to do.

I peeled down my coveralls and checked over my reflection. Today was a big deal. I realized that if Kevin were to get accepted to one of the colleges he'd applied to, there'd be no way in hell our father would support him, let alone pay for it. That was where I could step up. I didn't make more than pennies as a mechanic, and savings had never been something I figured I needed, but I was old enough. I'd never taken out a loan before, but it made sense that my first one would be to help put Kevin through school. The kid was damn near a genius, so I also hoped he could also get a few scholarships.

It has to be enough.

I straddled my bike and steadied my breath before pulling out into the warm June afternoon for my appointment at the bank.

WALKING into the small building that housed Perry Investments had my palms sweating. I dragged them across the thighs of my jeans and scanned the lobby. A few small offices with large windows lined the back wall, and a teller I recognized from town offered a friendly greeting. The lobby was small, but the exterior windows pulled in bright light, making the space seem bigger. The wood floors were old, but they'd been buffed to a high shine. I hadn't been inside the building in some time, but the recent updates and changes were evident.

Montana had seen an influx of rich families flocking to the rural areas for a more affordable cost of living or to "get in touch with nature" or some shit. First they overran Bozeman, and now they were spreading to the unclaimed rural counties. I fucking hated it. Most recently the branch of Chikalu Falls' little bank had been acquired and merged to include investment banking. Despite my disdain for changing our small town, if I had any hope of securing a loan, I had to play nice.

I did my best to hide a grimace.

Walking up to the counter, the young teller plastered a smile on her face, but her eyes flitted between me and the elderly officer sitting on the stool by the door, nearly asleep.

Jesus. I'm not here to rob the place.

"Good morning."

"Morning." Nerves tickled the nape of my neck. "I, uh, I would like to speak with someone about a loan."

Her owl eyes went wider. "Oh, yes. Um, well." She shuffled a few papers before dropping the pile on the floor. I peered over the counter to see her frantically scooping them up and muttering to herself.

"I've got this, Annabeth."

My eyes shot up to meet Charlotte's warm hazel gaze. Heat spread across my chest. Charlotte stood across the counter from me. Her black dress was high necked and modest but did nothing to hide the nip of her waist or the swell of her breasts. I willed my eyes to stay up.

"Good morning, Mr. Bailey."

Fuck, I like the sound of that.

I cleared my throat. "Good morning." I clamped my jaw down in an effort to control the wild thump of my heartbeat.

"Why don't you come this way?" She gestured toward one of the back offices as her smile widened. "Let's see how I can help."

I nodded and moved around the counter toward the offices. With Charlotte's back to me, I had an unobstructed view of her full hips and tight, round ass. My palm itched to smack it, and I wondered if Charlotte was secretly the kind of woman who liked that. When she shot a hot look over her shoulder and only smirked when she caught me looking, I bit my lip to keep from smiling.

Fuck. She just might be.

We entered her tidy office. Her desk was uncluttered, and her desk supplies were orderly and in their dedicated spots. The room was small and filled with her complex scent, which I'd gotten only a hint of at the bar. It was woodsy and bold, but also soft and floral. A dichotomy of masculine and feminine. A mystery—much like the woman smiling in front of me.

"Please, take a seat." She gestured toward the chair.

"After you." I may be poor white trash, but my mama would have been proud I remembered my manners.

Charlotte smiled again, and my heart rolled around in my chest. When she sat, I followed suit, rubbing my palms against the thighs of my jeans. For a beat, we sat there, staring at each other, and amusement danced in her eyes.

"I was hoping I'd run into you again."

Damn, I liked how assertive she was. Demure was not in her genetic makeup. I tried to play it cool. "In a town this size, it's bound to happen." Her eyes lowered at my dismissal.

Shit.

"I like running into you," I added.

She bit the inside of her lip to control the smile that twitched at the corners of her mouth. My leg bounced. This woman rattled my insides and made me want to crack open my chest and spill everything. She should know better than to be so open and sweet to a man like me.

Still radiating warmth, Charlotte asked, "So what can I help you with today?"

My stomach curled at the thought of airing out my family's dirty laundry. I hated that she was about to find out who I'd come from and the dead end that was my life. "I'm looking to get a loan."

She nodded slightly as she tipped her head. She lifted her hands. "Looks like you came to the right place." Charlotte opened a drawer and grabbed a small packet of papers. "I can help you with the application process. Will this be a business loan or a personal loan?"

"Personal." My skin felt too tight. I was at war with wanting to impress this girl, but I knew the more she knew about me, the faster she'd run. We started with the basics of the application. Charlotte nibbled her lip as she carefully entered the information. When we got to the nitty-gritty of assets— (*none*), credit— (*nonexistent*), and rationale— (*because I loved my brother*), she simply listened in quiet understanding. No judgment. My nostrils flared, but I was determined to look her in the eye. I knew full well that I was a risk for any bank willing to take a chance on me. I laced my fingers together to keep from fidgeting. Baring myself to criticism fucking sucked, but if I had to do it for Kevin, I would.

Charlotte gently placed her pencil down and smiled. "There are a lot of other factors to be considered when approving a personal loan."

"Risks." The stern voice over my shoulder had me whipping my head back. Standing in the doorway was a man in a sharp suit, his mouth turned down in a frown.

Charlotte popped up from her chair. "Mr. Bailey. This is Mr. Perry, the company president"—I stood to shake his hand as she continued—"and my father."

His eyes flicked down to the stains on my hands, and rather than slink away from his disapproving gaze, I squeezed his hand a fraction harder.

"As I was saying," he continued, "there are many factors to consider when approving a personal loan of this size. We'll be in touch."

Charlotte stiffened at my side, irritation radiating off her in waves. She lightly cleared her throat before smothering any outward signs of annoyance. "I still have a few questions for Mr. Bailey, and then I will happily escort him out."

Mr. Perry's only response was a quiet *hmm* dripping with disapproval. The look he shot me telegraphed his disdain, as though he was offended I even dared to breathe the same air as his daughter.

Charlotte stood proud, not backing down from her father's stare, though I did catch her rubbing her thumb against her finger. In her own way, she was standing up for me. *Odd.* I couldn't recall the last time that had happened. When Mr. Perry left, a whoosh of breath expelled from her lungs.

"I apologize."

I shrugged, not disagreeing with her father's assessment of me. "You said you had more questions?"

A shy smile, the kind that widened by the second, crept

across her pretty face. "Actually, no. I have all of the information that I need for the loan." She didn't move, but she looked at me expectantly.

Ask her out. Grow a pair and ask her out, asshole.

The words were lodged in my throat. I couldn't bring myself to do it.

"Thank you for your time today, Ms. Perry. I can see myself out." Without waiting for her response, I carried my shame on my shoulders and walked out of her office. I couldn't fuck this up for Kevin. My future, and the future of my little brother, lay at the feet of the most enticing woman I had ever met.

FIVE
CHARLOTTE

Matthew Bailey was quite possibly the most infuriating, complicated, and *sexy-as-hell* man I had ever met. It had been a shock to see his large strides eating up the distance between the entrance and the bank counter. He moved like a panther—muscular and dangerous and powerful. Every pair of eyes tracked his movements as he stalked toward Annabeth. I had practically bolted out of my office to intercept him.

He seemed tense and wary of divulging information for the loan application, but nothing he'd said was that big of a deal. On paper he was hardworking, albeit a bit old-fashioned, and he lacked any kind of credit to help prove he'd be a candidate for a personal loan. While I wouldn't make a special exception for him simply because my libido went haywire whenever I thought of him, it wouldn't be unheard of for a local branch to take a chance on someone.

My father had clearly disagreed. I was incensed at his rudeness and blatant dismissal of Matthew. He had no clue who Matthew was. Daddy simply saw dirty hands and denim. I didn't really know Matthew well, either, but there was something about him. Depth simmering just below the surface. My father's uppity attitude toward the residents of Chikalu Falls made me glad to know he would be returning to St. Louis the day after next.

Then you can run the firm as you see fit. Take chances on the people who deserve it.

The opportunity to do right by people was the only benefit to managing the branch. Investments and banking were not my lifelong dream. I was good with numbers, but nothing about it felt right. Like a sweater that fit just fine but was itchy and made you squirm.

I craved adventure. Newness. *Freedom.* A deep and longing part of me hoped that the fourteen hundred miles between Montana and Missouri would help free me from the cage my family had created for me. My wings were weak and unused, but they were ready.

I stared at the large garage bay doors from the inside of my car. My hands smoothed the packet of paperwork I was using as my excuse to seek him out early on a Monday morning. Inside the garage, a beat thumped low from a small speaker. A pair of legs stuck out from beneath a car. I used my vantage to check out where Matthew worked. His space was organized, though greasy and full of tools. A few other mechanics worked in adjacent bays, laughing and shouting mild insults at each other as they worked.

Matthew rolled out from under the car, his black boots coming to rest on either side of the red scooter thing on wheels. An image of me straddling his trim hips as he drove up into me flashed in my mind.

Get ahold of yourself.

I clenched my thighs together, relishing the dull ache that settled between my legs. After checking my makeup one last time in the rearview mirror, I pushed the door open and walked toward him before I chickened out.

A scowl morphed into recognition and surprise as I walked up. A low whistle sounded from someone to my left, but my eyes never left Matthew.

"Shut it," he barked.

"Hi." I could feel my smile was too eager, too wide, but I couldn't help it. He was so damn handsome with his mossy eyes and the way his greasy coveralls hugged his muscular frame.

Matthew pulled a rag from his back pocket and wiped his hands. "It's a surprise to see you here. Something wrong with your car?"

Warmth flamed my cheeks as I glanced back at my car. "No, actually. I'm sorry to bug you at work, but I just needed one last signature."

Lie. I could have easily gotten the signature at the office once his file was reviewed.

He eyed the papers and shifted his body weight, shielding them from the other guys at the shop, who were more invested in our interaction than in the work they had in their bays.

"'Course. No problem. What is it?"

I handed him the papers and a pen. "You just need to sign"—I pointed one manicured fingernail at the line —"here. Then I'll submit it along with my recommendation."

He paused and looked directly at me. "Thank you."

My skin warmed at his appreciation. If I hadn't decided before, I was definitely putting in an additional good word for Matthew Bailey. Besides, what better reason to approve a loan than to help his family?

He scrawled his illegible signature on the line and

handed the packet back to me. A smudge of grease darkened the corner. "Fuck." He grabbed his rag and scrubbed violently at his hands again. "Shit. I'm sorry."

I shrugged, though he looked nearly crestfallen, as though a tiny mark on the paperwork would be the deciding factor of whether we approved his loan request. "It's not a problem at all."

I waited a beat. Then another. "Okay." I swept my hair behind my ear. "You mentioned there's a lot more to Chikalu Falls than meets the eye. If the offer to show me something new is still on the table, I accept." Shocked by my own boldness, I was rooted to the ground.

His eyes searched my face, but he didn't speak. Embarrassment and panic rose up my spine. "All right, bye."

I swiveled on my heels, walking as fast as I could toward my car without actually breaking into a run. I wanted the pavement of the parking lot to open and swallow me whole. I paused at my car to breathe and raised my eyes to the sky.

If aliens are real, please take me now.

I was fumbling with my keys when I heard Matthew call after me. "Hey, wait up." I turned as he jogged toward me, and my heart thumped to the rhythm of his heavy footfalls. "I'm so sorry. That was rude."

I swiped a hand in the air. "No, I'm sorry. I just assumed, but . . . you know what? You were just being nice. It's not a big deal."

Matthew's large, calloused hand reached out to capture mine. "Stop. Please." The softness of my hand was enveloped in the roughness of his. I didn't miss the current that buzzed between us. "I would love to take you out."

I swallowed thickly. The softness in his eyes was alarming. That look was more dangerous than any scowl I'd seen on his face before. I smiled. "Just say when."

"Friday night. I can pick you up on my motorcycle, if that's okay."

It took every ounce of control not to squeal like a school-girl right there. Instead I clenched my jaw and willed my voice to sound calm. Cool. "That sounds perfect. I assume you remember where I live?"

SIX

MATTHEW

Though I would never admit it, I not only remembered where she lived but had taken to riding a different way home from work every day in hopes I'd catch a glimpse of her coppery hair and the flash of her gorgeous smile.

I have lost my mind over this woman.

By Friday night, my body was coiled tight. Thoughts of Charlotte clouded my mind and made doing almost anything else nearly impossible. She was light and fun, but I also detected a hint of boldness and resilience below the surface. I wanted to peel back her layers and see what made her tick. I also wanted to peel off the layers of her buttoned-up clothing to find what treasures lay there too.

I swallowed a groan as I pulled my hands through my hair. She didn't need some asshole sniffing around her like a dog, but *fuck*. If she kept shooting me those looks every time I passed her on Main Street, I was going to combust. Twice this week I had seen her around town. Her eyes, green and ringed with cinnamon, would meet mine, and a playful knowing danced between us. I'd tip my head and she'd smile, all the while my heart squeezing in my throat.

If I lasted five minutes without kissing her, it would be a goddamn miracle.

As I rode up her quiet street, the intense rumble of my exhaust bouncing off the quaint little houses, my palms started to sweat. Maybe Charlotte wasn't the kind of girl who appreciated hanging on to the back of a bike as it barreled down wide-open country roads—though I'd caught a gleam in her eye once or twice that told me maybe she was.

Charlotte's house came into view and my pulse skyrocketed. The house was small and simple, but clean. Similar to the other houses on the street, it was a ranch-style home with bright-white siding and deep-navy shutters. The house looked as though it had been empty for some time, and the flower beds running along the front of the house were overrun with weeds. My bike slowed as I turned up her driveway and parked.

I untucked a small bundle of flowers from beneath my shirt. I'd hoped it would help keep them from getting trashed by the wind, and despite being a little rumpled, they looked pretty good. My boots hit the pavement with confident strides, but my heart hammered wildly. An elderly neighbor checking the mail stopped to gawk. I nodded in greeting, but she clutched her jacket tighter and hustled back into her house.

Standing at Charlotte's doorway, I sucked in a deep breath and ran a hand down my stomach. I looked at the sad little wildflowers one last time, wishing I'd had the Chevelle to drive so they wouldn't have gotten so fucked up. I picked out a few broken stems, tossing them into the weeds. One last breath and I rang the bell. Within seconds the door pulled open.

She was waiting.

My smile grew wider. I lifted the sad-looking flowers between us. "Um."

Charlotte's mossy eyes met mine, and a smile split across her face. "Thank you! That's so sweet."

I cleared my throat and widened my stance. Unsure what to do with my hands, I clamped them in front of me. "You ready?"

"Yes! Let me just put these in water. Come in." She turned, and my eyes ran up the backs of her denim-clad thighs. The jeans hugged her curves and creased below her ass in the most sinful way. I worked my jaw to keep myself in check. Her billowy shirt was gauzy and fluttered around her waist as she walked into the kitchen. I liked that it was feminine and left a little to the imagination.

Charlotte's home was as tidy as I'd expected. Not really lived in yet, but organized. Other than a blanket thrown haphazardly on a chair with a book on the coffee table, nothing was out of place.

"Is your father home?" Despite his obvious dislike for me, I wanted the opportunity to shake his hand.

Charlotte turned. "They're gone for the weekend. My sister talked them into a shopping trip in Bozeman. It's just us."

My eyebrows lifted at her inclusion of *its just us*. Before I could respond, Charlotte turned. She grabbed a mason jar from the cabinet, filled it with tap water, and neatly arranged the blooms. The soft smile she gave the flowers made my chest tight. She placed the flowers on the sunny windowsill and turned.

"Now I'm ready."

I gestured toward the door. "Let's get to it then."

If I thought Charlotte's prim exterior would make her wary of my bike, I was dead wrong. Excited energy radiated off her as we approached the motorcycle.

"First time?"

She bit her lush lower lip and nodded. I swung a leg over and settled onto the bike, scooting forward to give her enough room. "There's not a lot of space. This seat's made for just one, but hang on and I'll keep you safe."

Charlotte piled her hair on top of her head in a bun and mounted my bike like an expert, her knees riding high on my hips. I swallowed a groan as she shifted forward, gluing her front to my back.

She fits perfectly.

Balancing our weight, I kick-started the bike and let the heavy rumble settle between my thighs. Charlotte's grip tightened around my waist. I laid a hand over her arm, pulling her tighter around my middle.

Over my shoulder I caught her wide grin and smirked at her. "Hang on."

Taking the long loop away from her home, I avoided downtown. I'm sure her elderly neighbor was already climbing the gossip tree and signaling that a Bailey was calling on the new girl in town. I knew well enough that until Charlotte was certain she wanted to be seen with me, I would do my best to help her save face. The small neighborhood gave way to open roads. I pulled my bike onto the wide pavement and let the warm summer air whip past us.

More than once, I spared a glance in her direction to make sure she was enjoying herself. Charlotte started off rigid and nervous but soon tipped her head back and closed her eyes, enjoying the floating, weightless energy of riding on a motorcycle. Her arms stayed firmly anchored to my abdomen, and I let one hand trail behind me, rubbing a small path up the side of her thigh and settling behind her knee. Her legs gripped my hips.

Goddamn this woman is something else.

Turning off on a quiet, dusty road, I reveled in how Charlotte leaned into me. I slowed the bike as we came to a clearing. The dense trees gave way to a small path that led down to the river. I planted my feet and steadied the bike as she dismounted. My mouth went dry as she shook out her hair, and her laughter floated on the warm summer air.

"What is this place?" She walked toward the small dock that jutted out from the riverbank. I worked to get the small paper sack out of the saddlebag.

"A quiet place." I tucked the items under my arm and led her toward the small pier. "It's peaceful."

She eyed me quietly as we walked in step toward the water. "You are full of surprises."

At the end of the pier, I sat, letting my long legs dangle off the side, and I arranged the small towel just behind us. "It's not much, but I thought you might want a snack after the ride."

A hunk of french bread from the café, some cheese and smoked meat. I hoped the small picnic was enough. "This is perfect!" Without hesitation, Charlotte tore a hunk of bread from the loaf and stuffed it unceremoniously into her mouth.

I laughed and did the same. Charlotte looked out onto the water. I couldn't help but watch her soak up the warm sun as it lit her face.

We laughed and talked. She asked questions about

Chikalu and told me about her friends in St. Louis. My hand grazed hers and heat pounded up my arm. When I captured her hand in mine, she didn't pull away. I tucked her hand on top of my thigh and held it there. She bumped her shoulder into mine and I grinned. I was smitten with this girl.

The moment was right, so I leaned into her, tipping her chin to angle her mouth toward mine. My lips captured hers, and a soft little moan breathed past her lips and into my mouth. My fingers snaked up her jaw and into her hairline. I gently pulled the back of her neck toward me, deepening the kiss. Charlotte's body moved with mine, melting into the kiss. Her hand went to my arm, anchoring it in place. My tongue dragged across hers, tasting mint and desire and heat. I broke the kiss before I did something really stupid, like pushing her down on the wood dock and covering her body with mine. My cock ached for her, but I wanted to give her more. Be better, *for her*.

My forehead rested against hers as we both fought to catch our breath.

"You are full of surprises, Matthew Bailey."

You make me want to be a better man.

The thought nearly flew out of my mouth, but I locked it down before embarrassing myself. Instead I simply grunted in response.

She smiled and looked out onto the water. "This is incredible. I had no idea places like this existed. Can you imagine living right here? A house right on the river with the mountains in the distance? It's so picturesque."

Truth was, I had never considered it. I never thought I'd live anywhere other than a rundown house or apartment on the shitty side of town, just like my father. But with her, I could already picture it. A big house, gardens, whatever the hell she wanted, I would bust my ass to make it happen.

"That sounds just about perfect." But I wasn't looking out onto the water like she was. Instead, I was memorizing the curves and lines of her face.

SEVEN

CHARLOTTE

MATTHEW BAILEY *WAS* full of surprises. After our simple but oh-so-swoony picnic date, my body was screaming for him to push me down onto the dock and fuck me right there in the early evening with the sun hanging low against the mountains.

He didn't.

Instead, we laughed and talked, and I was home at a respectable time. Trouble was, I really wanted to be disrespected when it came to Matthew Bailey. I wanted him to give in to the urges I saw simmering just below the surface. But, to my surprise, he was a gentleman underneath all that grease and grump.

"I would love to see you again." His eyes radiated warmth.

"How about tomorrow?" I toyed with my lower lip, knowing I sounded a bit overeager and hoping I wasn't being too forward.

"Tomorrow would be absolutely perfect."

We made our plans for the following night as my heart fluttered. He claimed to be able to show me something entirely new in Chikalu Falls, and I could hardly wait for the twenty-four hours to tick by. They slogged on torturously, but by six o'clock I was showered, smoothed, and thrumming with anticipation.

The knock at the door forced a surprised little yelp from me. I had been listening intently for the grumble and roar of his motorcycle. When I opened the door, Matthew looked up, all shy and devastating, with the smirk that made my insides warm and liquid.

"Evening, ma'am." His Western drawl flowed over me like warm honey. "Care for a ride?"

Matthew moved his shoulder to reveal a muscle car painted neon purple. My eyes went wide. "You didn't strike me as a purple man."

He stepped aside as I pulled the front door closed behind me and locked up.

"That"—he tossed a thumb over his shoulder—"is 'plum crazy' purple."

I laughed at the sheer absurdity. "It sure is something." I walked toward the car and Matthew followed me to the passenger side, opening the door for me and making sure I was secure before closing the door and rounding the hood.

There was something different about him. Excitement. Lightness. A flash of something mischievous crossed his features as he pulled out of my driveway and gunned the beast of a car down my street.

It took about an hour to reach wherever he was taking me, but the conversation was easy, and we laughed together in the small cab of the car. He asked about my life in St. Louis, if I missed it, and how I liked working for my father's business. I was honest and told him about how different Chikalu was, that I didn't really miss St. Louis, that my job felt like an obligation but also left me feeling unfulfilled. I talked about all the places I'd love to explore and visit. He nodded and listened. He also dreamed of travel.

"Where would you rather be?" I asked.

His large hand reached over and captured mine. "There's nowhere else I'd rather be than right here with you." My heart lurched in my chest.

We arrived at a large field with cars parked in neat rows. Matthew passed them all, went through another gate, and parked close to a dirt track. As we walked toward a stadium, a sign read The Gulch.

Tracking my eyes, Matthew clarified. "Ever been to a race?"

I shook my head. Surprise and nerves tickled my skin.

"You're in for it. The food is pretty good, the races are fast, and the crowd is a great time."

Matthew helped me out of the car, and when I took his hand, he kept it tucked in his. The air around the stadium was electrified and felt a little bit dangerous. I kept my body close to his as I looked around. The air smelled like fire, dirt, and engine oil. The wind from the mountains swept through, easing the thick smells of burned rubber and gasoline.

I smoothed a hand down my outfit. My crisp cotton shirt was sleeveless and tied in a cute knot at my belly button. The long blue-and-white skirt I'd chosen flowed down to midcalf. I'd picked it thinking that I could wear a pretty skirt but still be covered when I hopped on the back of Matthew's bike. In this crowd, I looked downright demure. Stuffy.

My eyes tracked in the crowd to a few women whose skirts looked more like oversize belts. Their midriffs were all exposed, and many had ornate tattoos snaking up their rib cages or down their arms. When Matthew noticed my attention on the women, he threw an arm over my shoulder and pulled me in closer.

"I got you." His deep voice echoed through me and helped to settle my nerves. Matthew cut through the crowd with purpose, and we didn't go unnoticed. People in town may shoot him wary glances, but in *this* crowd, it was like being on the arm of a celebrity. There were whistles and head nods and handshakes. Matthew could hardly get through the crowd without someone stopping him to say hello.

We eventually got to a small clearing where mostly trucks and a few cars were parked. Tailgates were down, and many had small grills going with food sizzling. One truck had a beer keg propped up on the bed and people lining up to fill their plastic cups. A lanky man ahead of us turned, his eyes pausing on me as he scanned the crowd. Appreciation filled his gaze as it raked down, then back up, my body. I crossed an arm in front of me. Beside me, Matthew watched my movement and his head whipped up.

Matthew's tense body language and the firm line of his mouth communicated loud and clear. *Mine.* A thrill danced up my spine.

The man nodded at me but addressed Matthew. "Sorry, boss."

Matthew stood taller, pulling me closer into his side as we slowly made our way up to the line toward the tailgate.

I peeked up at him. "Boss?"

He only grumbled in response, and before we could make it up to the front of the line, two other men approached, balancing cups and tinfoil-wrapped items.

"Ricky, what's up, man?"

Ricky smiled wide. "Can't have you waiting in line. Beers and dogs?"

Matthew started unloading the cups and small foil packages. He lifted a hot dog in my direction. "Hot dog okay?"

"Thank you."

The two men turned to look at me as I passed the warm foil packet between my hands. Matthew handed me a plastic cup of beer. "Ricky, Ansel, this is Charlotte. Charlotte, these boys are the best driving duo in the country."

The man named Ansel illuminated at the praise Matthew gave him. Ricky smirked and replied, "Best in the state, more like."

"It's nice to meet you both. Thank you." I lifted the hot dog in salute. We left the line, heading toward a concrete overhang that looked out onto the dirt track. My eyes moved up to the stadium seats. "Are we going up there?"

Matthew smiled, but Ricky cut in. "Shit. The best mechanic in four states doesn't sit with the crowd. Y'all get front-row seats."

The best mechanic in four states.

My chest swelled with pride for my date, despite the fact he seemed to ignore the comment completely.

Matthew whispered something to the men, and they walked away. He leaned closer, his warm leather scent warming my insides. "We may get a little dusty down here. I didn't think to mention it. We can sit higher if you'd rather."

I bumped my shoulder with his. "Well, we can't have the best mechanic in four states sitting in the crowd like a commoner, now can we?" I pursed my lips, trying to hide a smile when he caught my chin.

Kiss me. Kiss me.

Matthew leaned closer but only swept his thumb across my lips, leaving a buzz in its wake. When Ricky and Ansel returned, Ansel had a set of gigantic headphones in his hand. Matthew took them and placed them over my ears.

"Gets . . . should . . ." The muffled rumble of his voice was nearly impossible to make out.

"What?" I shouted.

The men chuckled, and Matthew pulled the headphones away from my ears. "I said, 'It gets loud, but these should help.'"

Then I placed them back over my ears and ran a hand down my thigh before looking out onto the track.

Tension built in my stomach. People waved to Matthew as they found a spot along the wall or up in the stands. "What are you, famous?" I tried to level my voice, but with the headphones on I was pretty sure I still shouted.

Matthew only lifted a shoulder and tossed me a wink. His hand rested on my knee, and I loved the warmth of his palm through the thin fabric of my skirt.

Before long, the first set of cars was lining up at the starting line. When the shot rang out, I could still make out the roar of the engines through the headphones. So loud, the rumble vibrated my chest. I couldn't look away as the cars sped off impossibly fast. The cars skidded and rounded the first corner. I pressed into Matthew's solid frame, my hand looping around his biceps. One car lost control and flew sideways into the concrete wall on the far end of the track. I squeezed tighter. Matthew leaned down, pressing his lips to my hair.

It was loud and dusty chaos. I loved it. My heart was pounding. The revving of the engines purred in my chest, and the breeze swirled with oil and earth and mountain air. Everyone was shouting for their favorite racer as the cars continued to make laps. The drivers raced hard, and their family and friends were there shouting encouragement.

When the cars made their final lap and a red car zipped over the finish line, I caught something cross Matthew's face. *Irritation, maybe?*

The action never slowed. As the first round of cars slowly lurched off the track, a new set began lining up for the next race. After a few minutes, a young man in driver's clothes walked up to us, looking bereft. Despite the noise, curiosity had me pulling the headphones from my ears.

He didn't acknowledge me but spoke directly to Matthew. "Something slipped. Timing belt maybe."

Matthew nodded. "Bring her up to the shop and I'll take a look at it."

Relief flooded the young man's face. "Will do. Thanks."

"You'll get him next time, Red."

The young man's face morphed into a rakish smile. "That's the plan." His eyes flicked to me, and he tipped his invisible hat before walking away.

"Friend of yours?"

"He's a good kid. He doesn't have a lot of money for repairs and upgrades, so I try to help him out. He's a real good racer. Actually has a chance at a few sponsorships. With a little help he can get out of this town."

I shook my head in disbelief. "You sure are something, Matthew Bailey."

He spun a finger in the air. "Is this all too much?"

I shook my head. "No way."

A deep, satisfied smile crossed his face as he pulled me closer to his side.

By the end of the fifth race, I was practically in Matthew's lap. I cheered and shouted for whichever car I liked—the purple one, the one with the shiny wheels, the female driver. When she crossed the finish line victorious, I shot to my feet, jumping and whooping and hollering. I collapsed next to him with a laugh, letting the headphones hang around my neck.

"Did you have a good time?"

"Are you kidding? The *best*! She was incredible!" I'm sure my smile was too wide, eyes a little too wild, but I couldn't help the bubble of energy that fizzed out of me.

"She's a great racer. Started out as a Powder Puff." I scrunched my chin and he continued, "Every month there's a Powder Puff race—amateur female drivers, usually the wives and girlfriends of the racers. It's a fun race, just a few laps and bragging rights if your old lady wins."

My eyes went wide, and I clamped my hands under my chin. "Please tell me that race is tonight."

A deep, hearty laugh had Matthew's head tipping back. It was the most beautiful sound in the world. "Slow down, Hurricane. It's not tonight, but if we didn't scare you off, I can get you behind the wheel."

We wound through the crowd, people stopping Matthew to make plans for repairs or to say their goodbyes. Matthew's long strides had us back to his car just as the cooler night air was settling in. Like a perfect gentleman, he opened my door and waited while I settled into the passenger seat. I did, however, catch the way his eyes raked up my legs and pause at the apex of my thighs.

Maybe not such a gentleman.

The buzz and excitement of the evening still thrummed in my veins. There was no way I could survive if Matthew dropped me off at my house with little more than a hug and a goodbye. As he folded his large frame into the car, heat crept up my neck. His thighs were thick, and I recalled how strong and warm they were beneath my hand. I wanted those thighs pressed against me while Matthew did naughty, dirty things to me.

I swallowed thickly as he pulled out of the parking lot and onto the quiet country road toward home. We talked idly, but my mind was wandering to dark and delicious places. Matthew may have been a bad boy on the outside, but he was also a gentleman. He needed a little nudge.

Slowly, I dragged one hand up my leg from my knee toward my thigh, letting my long skirt gather in my lap. Matthew's eyes caught the movement, and his breath hitched. He cleared his throat and adjusted in the seat.

"I had a great time tonight." I was pleased with how desire deepened my voice.

Sultry. Powerful.

Matthew's eyes glanced back to my lap. "I'm glad."

I continued brushing my fingertips against the bare skin of my legs, imagining it was Matthew blazing a trail up my thigh. "All the noise, the masculinity of it . . ." I squirmed in my seat. "I liked it."

"Oh yeah? How much did you like it?"

Feeling emboldened by the darkening desire that crossed his face, my hand disappeared beneath the heap of fabric of my skirt. "Feel for yourself."

His eyes left the road and shot to mine. I tipped my head back against the headrest, closing my eyes. Starting at my bare knee, Matthew's long fingertips gently moved up my thigh. My heartbeat hammered wildly, and my stomach clenched as he went higher. Dipping below the bunched material of my skirt, his featherlight touch grazed the mound of my pussy.

A soft moan escaped past my lips as his fingers stroked the outside of my panties. "Fuck, Lottie. You're soaked."

The use of a nickname had my knees clenching, capturing his wide hand between my thighs. My hands traced up my ribs and floated over my breasts. My nipples puckered to stiff peaks beneath the lace of my bra.

"Take them off." The coarse demand had my breath hitching. Matthew planted his hands on the steering wheel as he stared ahead at the road.

I looped my fingertips around the top of my panties and slowly slid them down, careful to give him a show as they dropped to the floorboard. I whispered my fingers across my throbbing pussy.

God, I want his hands there.

"Keep going," he demanded. "Finger your pussy while I watch."

Holy shit.

In the past, sex had always been straightforward, and certainly no one had ever watched me play with myself before. My arousal slicked between my thighs when I did as I was told. My eyes moved to the impossibly huge bulge straining against the front of his jeans. I licked my lips, and he groaned.

"Lottie. I said touch yourself. *Now.*"

On a soft moan, I dragged my fingertips up the seam of my soaking-wet pussy. I dragged the wetness through my folds and circled my clit. My hips bucked as I closed my eyes and imagined Matthew watching me, touching me. We flew down the quiet country roads as I continued to tease and dip one finger inside.

"Fuck, baby. You smell so fucking good. I can't wait to taste you."

The shock of his words had my desire peaking. Faster, I dipped one finger, then two, into my aching center. I imagined what it would feel like for him to tower over me, gaining entrance and stretching me open with his monster cock. As I reached my climax, Matthew's wide palm reached across and settled at the base of my neck. As he squeezed and massaged the muscles of my neck, I came undone. Over and over, my inner walls pulsed. My skirt was soaked, but I didn't care.

My breathing was ragged as my eyes fluttered open. Still too turned on to be embarrassed, I lolled my head to the side to look at Matthew's chiseled jawline. He shifted uncomfortably in the seat as his breaths came out in hard pants between gritted teeth. I looked again at the swell of his cock pressing against his jeans and bit my lower lip.

"Aw, handsome. Let me help you with that."

EIGHT

MATTHEW

"Aw, handsome. Let me help you with that." Charlotte's voice was husky as she unbuckled her seat belt. One touch of her soft hand to my cock and I knew I'd come. All night I had been holding back, trying desperately not to touch her too much. I wanted her to know she was special, respected. When we finally got to it, I needed her to know that she wasn't just some random fuck.

That was, until she started lifting her skirt and teasing her pussy. No man had that kind of control. Watching her hips swivel while her delicate fingers swirled around her clit was the most erotic and gorgeous thing I'd ever witnessed.

My erection was painful as I tried to focus on not crashing the fucking car. Charlotte's hand moved across my thigh and squeezed. Her fingers started working on the button to my jeans, and I shifted slightly to allow access. As she peeled down the zipper, my cock swelled further without the restriction of the denim.

"Jesus Christ," she whispered into the darkness.

A primal swell of pride filled my chest at the awe that laced through her voice. I focused on the road but stole a peek to see her delicate fingers wrap around my hard length. A surge of pressure strained against her hand, and heat pooled between my thighs.

Slowly, torturously, Charlotte started stroking my cock. A moan rumbled in my chest.

She whispered, almost tentatively, "You like that?"

"Fuck, Lottie. You feel incredible."

As if my words filled her with confidence, she gave my cock one firm, hard tug.

"Spit on it." My eyes immediately flashed to hers. A brief moment of panic that I'd gone too far, too fast, tightened my chest. Charlotte's lips curved into a sultry smile before she shifted in her seat and dipped her head toward my cock.

Oh fuck.

She licked her lips and let the spit pool and drip down her tongue and over my cock. Lowering her mouth, she laved the head of my cock with her tongue before closing her lips over the crown. I pulsed in her mouth.

I moaned her name, keeping my eyes pinned on the road. I fought the urge to thrust my hips up into her mouth.

"I like you telling me what to do." Her voice was breathy, and the warm air brushing against me only spiraled me higher.

I stroked hair away from her face as her eyes crinkled at the corners with a soft smile. She bent down again to take me between her lips, deeper than before.

"Relax your throat."

Her knees pinched together as a moan tore through her, vibrating her throat. She kept one hand firmly around the base of my cock, stroking me in time as she fucked me with that pretty little mouth.

"That's it, baby. Goddamn that feels good."

She popped her mouth off the tip. "Are you going to come for me?" She kept sucking and stroking. I was hurtling closer and closer to the edge, trying my damnedest to make it safely to her house.

"Grab your panties."

Charlotte reached for the discarded scrap of material between her feet on the floorboard. Balling the panties in her hand, she stroked me with the smooth fabric.

"Yes, yes," I moaned.

Charlotte leaned forward, pressing open-mouthed kisses along my jawline and neck. Tensions burst through me. My release pulsed, over and over, as she collected it in the silky fabric of her underwear, never stopping her assault on my neck.

I shuddered, the intensity of the moment not lost on me. When I peeled my eyes from the road, a wide, proud grin split her face.

"You're trouble." I laughed. She caught her lower lip between her teeth as I reached over to stroke a thumb down her cheek. I tucked myself back into my jeans as Charlotte did her best to smooth and right her skirt. If anyone had seen us, they would have known exactly what we'd been up to. Charlotte recognized it, too, because she nearly came unglued in a fit of giggles. The warm, tinkling sound of her laughter filled the car, and I couldn't help but laugh along with her.

A minute later I was pulling into her driveway. I watched as she balled the drenched panties into her fist. My heart clunked and my cock throbbed. "Sorry about that."

"Are you kidding? That was so hot."

Relief washed over me. As we got out of the car, I walked as slowly as I could, letting time drag out before I had to say goodbye. When we reached her door, she let out a soft sigh.

"Thank you for tonight. It was incredible."

I turned her and closed the space between us, Charlotte's back resting against the home's front door. Our breaths filled the quiet air.

"I'm glad you had a good time. And that ride home was . . . yeah." I smoothed her auburn hair from her face. "But you deserve a proper kiss."

Her breath hitched in her throat as I leaned my head down. Slowly, I moved my mouth over hers. Charlotte leaned into the kiss, arching her back to press into me. Every cord of restraint was pulled taut as I fought to keep the kiss tender. Tipping my head, I deepened the kiss, slanting my tongue over hers. We fit together. Her hands balled at the back of my shirt, and my hands cradled her head.

Charlotte had blown into my life in an unexpected whirlwind. A man who grows up with nothing can recognize when something good comes into his life. All at once she was everything. Right then I knew. She was it for me. I didn't deserve her. I had to find a way to become someone who did.

I broke the kiss and willed myself to step back and gaze down at her. Her lids were lax and dreamy. I wanted nothing more than for her to invite me in so I could spend the night tangled in her arms.

Three words used every ounce of willpower in my body. "Good night, Hurricane."

THE BUZZ of the shop radio filled the air as "Feel Like Makin' Love" by Bad Company crackled through the speakers.

Hell yeah, man. Same.

My thumb tapped the beat against my thigh as I examined the transmission in front of me. I was lucky I could think about anything other than Charlotte and last night at the racetrack.

"Someone got laid last night. You take Miss Prim and Proper home after the race?"

"Fuck off." No one was going to talk shit about Charlotte, but once his back was turned, I couldn't help but smirk. The guys at the shop could bust my balls all they wanted—I was fucking elated, and no one could take that away from me.

I was about to make it clear that if he spoke ill of her again, he'd feel the brunt of my fist, when the boss called out from the office.

"Bailey. Call for you." Hope bloomed in my chest.

Would she call me at work?

A strange excitement ran down my back. I tried to play it cool as I walked through the shop into the small office. My boss stayed in the lobby, gesturing toward his office.

"Hello?"

"Matt."

My stomach dropped out. "Kevin. What's wrong?"

The line was quiet, and a thousand terrible thoughts raced through my mind. Finally, he spoke up. "It's . . . I just need a little help at the house."

"I'm on my way." I slammed the phone down and barreled out of the office. Already walking out the door, I shouted over my shoulder to my boss. "I have to go."

He balked, but I didn't give a shit. Hopefully tomorrow I'd still have a job, but if I didn't, there was always another shop.

My motorcycle sped down the winding mountain road toward the rundown houses on the edge of town. The homes got closer together and significantly more depressing looking. When I pulled up to the house I grew up in, I immediately saw the problem.

The front door was kicked in, wood splintered and the frame busted. When I entered, I took in the chaos around me. Shattered glass, an upturned table, Kevin's schoolwork strewn across the floor. He was on his hands and knees, scrubbing something on the kitchen linoleum.

My pulse hammered. Rage filled my gut, but when his eyes met mine, I softened.

"Thanks for coming." His voice was filled with sadness.

I didn't reply but walked to him, the glass crunching beneath my boots. I pulled him off the floor and into a hug. Relief made his shoulder go slack.

"Let's get this cleaned up."

In silence, we cleaned up the mess. It wasn't the first time our father had lost control and we'd been left to deal with the aftermath. He'd been doing it most of our lives. I looked around the cramped space. When Mom's laughter had faded and she was gone, it had turned into a prison. Those four walls had seen enough, and it was a good thing they couldn't talk. If it weren't for Kevin, I'd be half tempted to burn the house to the ground.

I gestured toward the broken door. "Forgot his keys again?"

He only nodded.

"You can't live like this."

Kevin turned to avoid my eyes. "Thanks for your help."

"I'm serious, Kev. You can't stay."

"It's not always like this. There are mostly good days. Really."

"We can't keep cleaning up his messes and acting like this isn't happening. Fine, so there are some good days, but what about the bad ones?" I gestured around the small living room. "What about when he loses control and trashes the place? Or worse? He turns his anger on you, and I won't stand for it. What about school?"

"What about it?"

I pinned him with a glare. "You know damn well I'm talking about Montana State."

Kevin shook his head and stared at his shoes, but I didn't miss the glimmer of hope that was there at the mention of the university.

"You've already done the hard part by being accepted and earning a scholarship. I'll help with the rest of the money."

"Matthew, I can't. What'll happen if I go? I can't give up on him too." The air sucked out of my lungs. I hated to admit it, but he was right. I had given up on helping my father a long time ago. The only reason I even stayed in Chikalu Falls was to be around for Kevin.

I knew more than ever I had to find a way to get him out of that dead-end town. He deserved so much more than walking on eggshells in the house, hoping Dad was having a decent day.

I put my hand on his shoulder and squeezed. "It'll get better. I promise."

After saying goodbye, I rode back to the shop to apologize and explain myself to the boss and try to make up for leaving so unexpectedly. I would continue to save my money and help pay for Kevin's tuition in the fall. It would be enough. It *had* to be enough. I thought back to Charlotte and the loan and hoped I hadn't just lied to my brother.

NINE

CHARLOTTE

"Hмм." A line of irritation deepened across my father's forehead.

Fantastic.

I remained still, knowing any amount of fidgeting would only annoy him further and delay his leaving Chikalu Falls.

He shuffled a few papers while he sat behind *my* desk to look over my work before he and my family returned to St. Louis. "You'll need to close out these accounts before the end of the month."

"Yes, sir."

He thumbed through a stack of files. I knew Matthew's application and paperwork were tucked in that stack, and my heart stuttered. As though he could read my thoughts, my father stopped on his file. Flicking it open, he glanced at the name across the top before flipping it closed again. In a swift move, he dumped the entire file into the trash.

I looked on, horrified. When he caught my eye, his tone was stern. "Charlotte. Our reputation is at stake here. We expanded to this town to serve a very specific clientele.

Businesses. All of the Montana transplants who need guidance on what to do with their finances. You understand."

I glanced at the trash basket. "Surely there's room to serve the community."

My father smoothed his fingers over his top lip. "You will run this branch as I see fit or I will find someone else who can. Davis is more than capable of running this firm."

It took every ounce of discipline to not tell him he could take the job and shove it up his ass. Davis was working in the Montana office with me and he could have it all.

All I'd ever wanted to do was make my parents proud of me—be pleasant and accommodating. Do the right thing. Trouble was, what felt like the right thing was in direct opposition to my father.

Pacify him and get him out the door. Figure it out later.

I steadied my smile. "I won't let you down, Dad."

Satisfied that I was rightfully back in my place, he sighed and pushed away from the desk. He stood aside and opened his arms. "Get in here."

I slipped inside his embrace. It was rare my father showed affection, but when he did, it was warm and strong. Tears pricked at my eyes.

"I'll miss you guys."

He squeezed me tighter. "Don't forget you're a Perry. There's nothing you can't handle."

When we left the cocoon of my office, I walked my father to the door, and the man shook my hand before leaving.

Ever the businessman.

Before he'd even made it to his car, my heels clipped against the wood floor of the lobby as I scurried back to my office. When I pulled Matthew's file from the trash, I smoothed my hands over the papers. His serious face with kind eyes filled my mind. My father would be pissed to know I had directly gone against his orders, but it would be weeks if not longer until he would be back to check in.

I dug through the drawer. I took a deep breath and pressed the rubber stamp across the top of the paper.

Approved.

"I THINK I'm going to puke." I doubled over and huffed out a breath.

"Relax. You already know what his dick tastes like. What's the big deal?" Trina's comment was dripping with laughter, and I couldn't help but giggle with her. I had confided in Trina after Matthew and I got hot and heavy in his car. It was so out of character for me, but I found he pushed my boundaries and made me want to do all kinds of delicious and dirty things.

"Listen, the house looks great, you're shaved and as smooth as a baby seal's ass. You're ready to go."

I smiled at my friend. Trina was the ultimate hype woman, and my confidence was growing by the second.

I looked over her handiwork in the mirror as Trina packed her makeup into a small tote bag. "I still can't believe you're sleeping with Matthew Bailey."

"We're not sleeping together." Heat rose in my face and added a pretty color to the blush Trina had swept across my cheekbones.

"Pfft. Okay. Maybe not *yet*."

My smile grew. I had a pretty good feeling that after our last date, dinner and a movie at my house would lead to the bedroom. Still, it bothered me that even Trina thought poorly of Matthew.

"He's a good guy. A gentleman. There's a softness underneath that hard exterior."

"If you say so." She lifted her shoulders and looked at me. "Just be careful."

"Thank you for helping me get ready tonight."

Trina wrapped me in a hug and squeezed. "You're my new favorite person. I'm so glad that you moved here."

I squeezed her back. Having a friend like Trina made life in Chikalu so much better.

She stepped away and dug out a small parcel from her bag. "Here. This is for you."

I took the soft tissue paper that was wrapped in a small rectangle. Slowly, I started to unwrap the package. As I peeled away the layers, a sliver of emerald green peeked out. I traced my fingertips across the silky fabric before pulling it up.

I held a bra with the softest lace I'd ever felt—and stared. The lace cups were so thin you could see right through them. There was no doubt that the low cups combined with the sheer fabric would leave very little to the imagination. The matching panties were just as gauzy. The center dipped low, and the straps would ride high on my hips. The single strip of fabric running up the back would have my ass—*my whole ass*—on display for Matthew.

My eyes went wide, and I covered the lingerie with my hands, embarrassment tingling at the base of my scalp.

Trina only smiled, completely unashamed to be giving me the most erotic pair of underwear I had ever *seen*, let alone owned.

"Against my better judgment, when I saw this, I knew

you had to have it. With your hair, the green will be perfect."

A flutter, low in my belly, went wild as I imagined Matthew's reaction to the undergarments.

"Trina. I—thank you. It's perfect."

She planted her hands across her wide hips. "I see a woman and I know exactly what kind of lingerie will make her feel incredible." She shrugged. "It's a gift. Matthew Bailey can thank me later." She winked and walked toward the door.

We hugged one last time, and I gripped her arm and squeezed. "I don't deserve you."

"You deserve the world, Charlotte. Don't forget that."

Forty minutes later, I was pacing my small living room and fanning my armpits.

Don't sweat. Don't sweat. Don't sweat.

A soft knock at the front door had me jumping and breathless. I smoothed a hand over the soft curls Trina had put in my hair and took a steadying breath before opening the door.

Matthew stood tall, feet planted, at the entrance. Every nerve ending tingled with awareness. When our eyes met, Matthew smiled. "Evening, Lottie."

My chest squeezed and my stomach clenched. He smelled clean and handsome, like he had maybe even added a hint of cologne just for me. His dark denim looked new and was slung low on his hips. I couldn't wait to sneak a view of how they hugged the curve of his ass. His dark Henley shirt was fitted, and the way the fabric strained against his biceps was sinful.

"Please, come in." I sounded breathy and a little too formal. My nerves were getting the best of me.

Get your shit together. Remember what Trina said— you've had your mouth on him. This shouldn't be a big deal.

"I wasn't sure what you liked, but I got this for you." Matthew held out a bottle of red wine as he walked into my house.

I grabbed the bottle and hugged it to my chest. "This is perfect." I led the way toward my kitchen. "I don't cook." I laughed. "But Francesca's does takeout. I hope that's okay."

"Perfect. How can I help?" Matthew ran his hands down his hips and tucked them into the front pockets of his jeans.

God, I want those hands on me.

"Um . . . let's plate it all up, and then we can eat." I was moving toward the small countertop when Matthew's body crowded my space. His large, warm hand cupped the back of my neck, his fingers tangling into the fine hairs at the nape of my neck.

Towering over me by several inches, Matthew pulled my body into his. My breath caught as he lowered his mouth to mine. Gentle at first, Matthew's mouth teased mine, pressing a soft kiss to my lips. Desire flooded my system, and I leaned into his frame, pinning my body against his. Slanting his mouth over mine, he deepened the kiss, teasing my mouth with his tongue. When I opened for him, he pulled me tighter against his chest and ground his hips into me. My nipples hardened against the lace of my bra, and they ached for his hands.

Matthew slowly released me, and I looked up at him. His stormy green eyes held me as a charged silence stretched between us. "I've been thinking about that mouth all day."

I sucked my bottom lip into my mouth to suppress my grin. His eyes were dark and wanting, like he was starving for me. I was just as hungry, and it had nothing to do with the Italian takeout on my counter.

Dinner can wait.

I rushed forward, wrapping my arms around his neck. His warm breath sent goose bumps erupting across my skin. On my tiptoes, I pulled his mouth to mine as I slid one hand down his abdomen to find his erection straining against his jeans. He hissed in a breath and pushed his hips forward, pressing into my palm. I gripped him through the denim as a hot, low need throbbed between my legs.

"Jesus, Lottie. I'm trying to be a gentleman here."

My fingers threaded through his hair as I kissed him harder. Breaking free, I brushed my lips against the shell of his ear. "Who said I wanted a gentleman?"

As shocked by my boldness as I was, Matthew reached behind my thighs and hiked me up onto the counter. His hands gripped my ass as he sucked and kissed my neck. He lowered his head down to my breasts, finding the sharp points of my nipples through the silky fabric of my top. His teeth scraped against the delicate skin, my entire body on fire.

He pulled back to look at me. I was certain my makeup was ruined and my lips were swollen from his demanding kisses. Matthew dragged the pad of his thumb across my tender lip. "You are the most gorgeous woman I have ever met."

Sudden shyness had me lowering my lashes. "Thank you."

Matthew stepped forward, spreading my legs to accommodate his hips. My center throbbed, aching to be filled. "Matthew," I said, "dinner can wait."

Without another word, he hauled me up, wrapping my

legs around his middle. With long strides, he stomped toward the back of the house.

Excitement danced through me. "Go left!" I shouted, hoping he'd make it to my bedroom before I combusted. Once inside my room, Matthew deposited me on the bed and quickly covered my body with his.

"Tell me, Lottie." He braced himself above me, looking deep into my eyes. "Tell me what you want and I'll give it to you."

I tightened my legs and squeezed my thighs around his hips. "You. I only want you, Matthew Bailey."

He pressed his hips into me, desire flickering across his features. Reaching down, he took one of my hands in his and raised it to his chest, placing it over his heart and covering it with his. "Do you feel that?"

His heart hammered against my palm. I swallowed hard and nodded.

"It's never been like this for me. With anyone."

I didn't realize how much I needed that. I needed to know that I wasn't just another notch on the bedpost of the town bad boy. I needed to know that this meant as much to him as it did to me.

Matthew reached into the pocket of his jeans and took out a condom. He tossed it on the bedside table and sat back on his heels. Sprawled beneath him, I stared up, aching to feel his warmth again.

Slowly, I started to unbutton my top. As the fabric fell away, Matthew traced the swell of my breasts with his fingertips, circling the taut bud of my nipples. His eyes drank up the lingerie that had been hidden beneath my shirt.

"Where the fuck did you find something like that in Chikalu?"

"It's a girl's secret."

He growled as he stared down at me. "Green's my favorite color." Matthew reached behind him to pull off his Henley. His chest and shoulders were broad, and his abs so cut it was unreal. I trailed my hand down the soft smattering of hair that lined his chest and stomach and disappeared behind the denim of his jeans.

He made quick work of removing the rest of my outfit, tossing my skirt and top on the floor beside the bed. I reached behind me to remove my bra as he slowly ran his hands along the side of my thighs and hooked his fingers around the band of my panties, peeling them down my legs. He stroked and massaged and kissed as he left me completely exposed beneath him. Matthew's chest was warm against my cool skin. My fingers raked across the peaks and valleys of the muscles on his back.

I moved my hands to undo his pants as quickly as I could. He helped to push his jeans and boxer briefs down, his cock springing forward between us. The anticipation was agony. Matthew rubbed his crown through my slick folds and circled my clit with the hot tip.

My back was lifting off the bed, urging him to push forward and consume me. Matthew reached toward the table, ripping the condom wrapper open with his teeth before rolling it down the length of his shaft. He squeezed the base before looking into my eyes.

Nerves rattled inside me as I thought about him splitting me open. "You're really big."

A cocky smile tugged at the corner of his mouth. "It'll fit. You'll take all of this cock and beg for more."

His bold statement had my pussy going, if possible, even more slick for him. He centered himself at my entrance before looking at me again. "Slow and deep? Or hard and fast?"

Oh fuck.

All of it. I wanted it all. "Slow and deep. Then hard."

With one hand braced against my thigh, pushing my legs wider, and one at the base of his cock, Matthew settled his hips against me as he pushed inside. Inch by scandalous inch, he stretched me until he was seated within.

I was so full.

Stuffed.

My inner walls fluttered around him as I adjusted to his size. After a moment, my hips moved with a greedy need for more. "Move, Matthew. I need you to move."

Slow and deep he pushed me closer and closer to the edge. As my clit rubbed against the base of him, I needed more. I wanted him to ravage me.

"Fuck me hard, Matthew. I'm ready."

As though I'd unleashed a beast, he pulled back and slammed into me. Thrust after hard thrust, he rocked my body. Matthew wrapped an arm around my back as he completely consumed me. Never in my life had I been fucked so fiercely. So raw.

A rush of heat passed through me as he found a rhythm that hit the deepest part of me. My entire body shook as I came around him. Going deeper still, spearing me into the mattress, Matthew's cock began to pulse as he came inside me. Its intensity was unlike anything I'd ever experienced.

As we both finished, we panted and tried to catch our breath. Our groans of pleasure filled the air. I lay under him, a boneless pile of nerve endings as he slowly kissed up my neck and across my jaw.

"Mmm." I couldn't even find words.

"Hey," he said softly.

When I opened my eyes, Matthew was looking down at me.

"Be my girl?"

My tongue pressed to the roof of my mouth to fight the surge of emotion rushing to the surface.

I was losing myself in this complicated, brooding loner of a man. I didn't trust my voice not to crack, so I swallowed hard.

"Always."

TEN
MATTHEW

LOOKING at Charlotte across the dining room table had my stomach tied up in knots. The soft glow from the kitchen light had fire dancing in her auburn hair and illuminated the depths of her expressive eyes. When she laughed, it was the most beautiful sound I could imagine. I wanted to find a thousand ways to light her up and hear it again.

In the haze of the most incredible sex of my entire life, I'd asked her to be my girl, and she hadn't turned away. Hadn't even hesitated. Defining these growing feelings inside me had been plaguing me for days. For some reason I couldn't explain, I needed to hear her say it. To acknowledge that whatever was forming between us wasn't a figment of my imagination and that she felt something too.

When she didn't even hesitate, my mind went blank. I'd never experienced unrestrained acceptance in that way. At least not since my mother and certainly not from any of the women I'd taken to bed. Most women saw my pissed-off exterior as some sort of challenge. My Lottie was different. She looked at me like she really saw me—the real me that had been buried so deep by stress and regret and anger.

"Hey, where'd you go?" Charlotte's brow was creased and her voice quiet as she cut into my thoughts.

I reached across the table to roll her hand around with mine. "I'm here. Lost in thought, I guess."

"Good thoughts, I hope."

"The best." I smiled, though a ghost of fear snaked through me. Fear that I didn't deserve any of this. That it was all too good to be true. "Your house is really nice." I looked around the immaculate space, trying to deflect the conversation.

"Thanks. It's okay, I guess."

Okay?

The house was spotless. A decent-size kitchen that opened into the living room. There was enough space for a small family to have a great home. I dreamed of houses like that as a kid. A house where I could invite friends over and not be embarrassed by the smell or worry that my dad would come home drunk and pissed off.

She's used to this—more than this, really. More than you can give her.

I buried the thought. I couldn't let my hang-ups ruin our night together.

After polishing off the reheated Italian food, we settled into the plushy couch for a movie. After clicking through the channels and not landing on anything, I decided to distract her by letting my fingers dance featherlight touches across her skin. Before I knew it, she was straddling my hips and riding me until she soaked us both as she came again.

Sated and exhausted, a movie played quietly in the background. I moved my hand around hers as our fingers laced and unlaced. The soft thin skin of her hand was a stark contrast to the rough, scarred surface of my own.

Charlotte's finger traced the intersecting lines on the

back of my hand. "You know, when I first saw you at the bar, your hands were all cut up. Trina said you were dangerous. A brawler. Now look at you."

I remembered the night she showed up at the Dirty Pidge. She was so hot in her short little dress. "I don't fight. Not if I don't have to."

My voice was a little too gruff, so I cleared my throat to dislodge the lump that had settled there. I had an insatiable need to open up to her—to crack my chest open and reveal every dark and depressing secret that lay inside.

"If you don't fight, how did your hand get so cut up?" she teased. Worry creased her forehead as she shifted to look me in the eyes as the atmosphere shifted.

"My father. He has a problem with alcohol. It makes him angry. For a long time he only cared about punishing himself." I scrubbed my hand across my face. If Charlotte was agreeing to be my girl, she deserved to know the truth about where I came from. "When I was little, I was too scared to fight back. I took the brunt of it for a long time. Now only Kevin is in the house, and I'm a lot bigger. My father needed a reminder that if he touches Kevin again, it's me he'll deal with."

Water pooled in her dark eyes. "Oh, Matthew . . ."

I pulled her closer, dropping a kiss on the top of her rumpled hair.

"I don't need you to feel sorry for me."

"What can we do?"

We.

Fuck. Her words hit me straight in the chest, knocking the wind out of me. "I've tried to get Kevin to leave, but he won't go. He's convinced Dad will change. The best bet is to help him make it out to Montana State."

Her hand gripped my forearm and squeezed as she settled back into me. "Then that's what we'll do."

Charlotte made it all sound so simple. In the quiet of the living room, I let her warmth seep into me and settle into my bones. Despite the movie in the background, Charlotte dozed, sprawled across my body. We were as close as two human bodies could get, and I fought the urge to pull her even closer. It was bliss. As I sat in the darkness, stroking the soft skin of her back, I'd come to a decision.

I kissed the top of Charlotte's head and she barely stirred. "I've been thinking," I whispered into the darkness. "Somehow I'm going to have to become the man you deserve, because I don't think I'm going to be able to live without you now."

Every fiber of my being knew it—if ever there was a girl worth stepping up for, it was her.

THE NEXT MORNING, it nearly killed me to leave. After twenty minutes of making out on her front porch, I had to force myself to pull away and get onto my bike. Charlotte waved as I rode down her street, and the sight of her bright smile on the porch as I pulled away hit me square in the chest.

She's home to me.

Back at my apartment, everything seemed grayer. Dirty.

I dug through my pocket, tossing my keys on the table and holding the delicate necklace in my palm. In the morning over breakfast, Charlotte had retreated to her bedroom, excitement radiating off her as she bounced back toward me and sat right on my lap.

"I want you to have something." She held up a slim

silver chain. Hanging from it was a small round piece of metal. One side was the face of an antique silver coin, and the other side was etched with an intricate, swirling script. Her initials—CAP.

I took it from her and examined it carefully.

"It's called a love token," she explained. "Back in the eighteen hundreds, love tokens were given as a memento or good luck charm. One side is the coin." *She turned the necklace over in my hand.* "And the other is hand engraved with the overlapping initials of your loved one. It's a symbol of growing love."

I smoothed the small round metal with my fingers. She'd looked so sweet and nervous when she'd given it to me. I may not be one for jewelry, but I hooked it around my neck and tucked the delicate chain into my shirt.

My heart ached for her.

Feeling lighter than ever, I scanned my cramped apartment.

This won't do.

I needed more, for myself and for Charlotte. Somehow, I needed to give her the life she deserved. I needed options.

On the wall, my phone rang twice before I reached it. "Hello?"

"Mr. Bailey. Gregg Morgan."

"Yes, sir." My palms felt clammy, and a shiver of unease coursed through me.

"I'll be passing through Chikalu Falls before heading back to the main office in Billings. Just confirming we're still on for our appointment at two."

Fuck.

"Yes, sir."

"Fantastic. I'll meet you at the satellite office."

Deciding to take the Chevelle, I cruised through downtown toward the small, rented office that served as the recruitment center for our county. Despite the midday hour, a familiar figure walked toward the main entrance to the Dirty Pigeon.

I hauled my car to the side of the road, not caring I wasn't in a parking space, before storming up the sidewalk.

"Lee."

My father's head whipped around, his eyes glazed and unrecognizing.

"Go home."

His jaw clenched as his head bobbed. It was clear he'd already been drinking. He spat a wad of chaw at my feet. "The fuck you think you're talking to?"

"Dad. You're done. It's time to go."

Anger flared across his features. His finger wagged in my face. "Don't you tell me when I'm done, you worthless piece of shit. You left us. Just like that worthless mama of yours."

I had started to turn when his eyes dropped to the small silver chain peeking out from my collar. He reached out, hooking a finger around the chain and pulling it from underneath my shirt before I could pull away.

"Look who's fancy."

I bristled at his invasion of my space. "It was a gift."

"Gift like that is awful expensive." He sucked his teeth. "So I guess the rumors are true."

My eyes slitted as I pinned him with my stare.

He shook a finger in my direction. "Yeah, they're true." He laughed. "Word around this shithole is you got yourself a taste of that rich-bitch pussy."

My fist clenched, and I ached to slam it into his face to shut him up. I ground my molars, willing myself to not let him get under my skin and make a scene in the middle of downtown.

"Ah, don't get so worked up. It won't last. With your dead mama and me." His arms spread wide. "We're in your blood whether you like it or not."

I shook my head. There was no reasoning with him when he was already half in the bag. I turned to walk away.

"I feel bad for her, really," he called after me.

I spun on my heels and surged into his space, lowering my face to his. "Stop. Talking."

He wavered on his feet, both hands in the air in front of him. "I'm just tellin' truths. You come from nothing. That's all you'll ever be. *Nothing.*"

"Fuck you."

"I'm just sparing you a lot of heartache here, kid. I'm gonna let you in on a little secret. Enjoy it while it lasts, because you're not the one she'll choose. A Bailey?" He scoffed. "You might as well tie an anchor around her pretty little neck and shove her into the water."

Too stunned to move, I watched my old man walk away and into the bar. Years of practice ensured he didn't sway, but I recognized the lazy, drunken hitch in his walk anyway.

ELEVEN
CHARLOTTE

I was in love with Matthew Bailey.

It may have happened fast, but there was no denying it. Everything inside of me called to him, and I couldn't pretend the connection between us wasn't real and deep.

I had never met, let alone dated, anyone who was so unapologetically themselves. Matthew was rough and sweet, serious and kind, funny and intense.

Matthew Bailey was *everything*.

I knew I had to thank Trina for the magical powers of her lingerie. Matthew had, quite literally, been eating out of my hands, and all the ways he'd worshipped my body were downright sinful.

A gentle moan escaped my lips as I became lost in memories of him.

The work hours seemed to drag, but the pep in my step helped me keep a positive attitude. Matthew and I agreed to meet for dinner midweek—neither of us could stand the thought of going another day, let alone wait until the weekend, without seeing each other. My foot tapped as I watched the clock. By lunchtime, I was crawling out of my skin in anticipation.

As five o'clock rolled around, I was still swamped with work. Tense and sweaty, I was racing the clock to organize and file the paperwork from several new accounts.

"You got somewhere you need to be?"

I looked up from my desk to see Davis standing in my doorway. "Um, actually, yes. I'm trying to get out at a decent hour tonight."

He looked at me, lips slightly pursed. "Hmm. That's too bad. I thought maybe we could order in some food and hammer out the last of the new accounts."

"I'm sorry, I can't." I shuffled the papers and did my best to keep the edges crisp as I shoved them into a file folder.

"Rain check?" Davis crossed his arms and smiled in my direction.

Oh shit. Is he hitting on me?

I blinked a few times. I had never thought of Davis in that way. He was nice enough and not bad to look at, but too stuffy. Buttoned-up.

Exactly the type of man my father would love for me to date.

"I'm sorry, Davis. I'm seeing someone."

His eyes widened and he straightened. "Is that so?" He hid his surprise behind a cool smile as he smoothed the front of his shirt. "I apologize, Charlotte. Your father hadn't mentioned it."

My hand flew to my hair to smooth a stray strand. Feeling awkward about having this conversation with a work colleague, I also wanted to scream that my father had nothing to do with my personal life. But the words died on my tongue. "Um. It's new."

He glanced at the stack of papers on my desk. "Listen, why don't you get out of here. I can finish filing that paperwork."

Hope bloomed in my chest. Davis was more than capable, and over the past few weeks we had shared several accounts. In fact, he could easily run the branch, and had I not been the daughter of the president, he likely would have. "Thank you! That would be so helpful."

I piled the remaining papers and shoved them toward the end of my desk as Davis scooped them up and turned toward the door.

I quickly logged out of my computer and threw my purse over my shoulder. As Davis walked through the threshold, he turned. "And when you get over that guy," he said, "maybe we can get that dinner."

Before I could set him straight that there would be no *getting over that guy*, he was gone.

I hurried home to freshen up before Matthew would be over. I decided that I would try my hand at domesticity and attempt to cook dinner. My eyes flew to the ceiling.

Please don't let me fuck this up.

After a quick shower, I followed the taco casserole recipe exactly. It looked and smelled edible as I slid it into the oven and waited. Matthew and I had agreed to meet at six thirty, but as the minutes ticked by, there was still no sign of him. By seven o'clock, the casserole was done, and Matthew was still not there.

What if something happened? What if he got into a wreck on his motorcycle?

Fear gripped my chest as I imagined him hurt, or worse, on the side of the road. Matthew wasn't the kind of man to stand a woman up. Something was very wrong.

Covering the dish with foil and taking it with me, I grabbed my purse and headed toward town. Matthew had told me where he lived, so I headed in that direction, driving slowly so I could scan the side of the road on the way.

Relieved but still uncertain, I saw no sign of him. When I pulled up to his apartment, Matthew's motorcycle was parked outside. A tiny shot of hurt pinched below my ribs.

Had he forgotten?

I balanced the casserole in my arms and lifted one hand to knock on the faded wooden door. When it pulled open, I smiled brightly. "Surprise!"

Matthew's eyes didn't light up the way they usually did. Instead, he looked tired. Upset. *Angry.*

"Hi!" I willed my voice to steady under his stare. "Maybe I misunderstood, but I thought we had plans to meet today."

Matthew dragged his hand down his face and sighed. His hair was a mess, like he'd dragged his hands through it a thousand times. "Damn it, Charlotte. I'm sorry. We did." He breathed another heavy breath. "The day got away from me."

I hoisted the dish a little higher. "No worries. I brought dinner to you."

"Yeah, come on in." He stepped aside to let me into his home.

The space was very small. Simple but tidy. The lack of furniture screamed *bachelor pad*, and the entire space was filled with the warm, comforting smell of him. I turned and smiled. "Great place."

A low grumble was his only response. He took the casserole dish from me and set it on the stovetop. Matthew braced his hands on the counter with his back to me, his head hung low.

My heart tumbled in my chest. I walked up behind him and smoothed a hand up the muscles in his back. "Hey, what's going on?" I asked softly.

Matthew turned and gathered me in his arms. He was strong and warm. I melted into him as he clung to me.

"It's been a rough week. A few days ago, I got into it with my father." I looked up to see Matthew shake his head and clench his jaw. "I found out that he went home that night and took it out on Kevin."

I sucked in a breath. "No . . . what happened? Is he okay?"

"He's fine. It was mostly words, a few broken dishes, and a shove or two, but Kevin is safe now." Matthew clenched his fist like he wanted to punch something. He tipped his head toward the back of the apartment. "He's sleeping in my room."

My eyes landed on the closed door, and my heart twisted. I had never met Kevin, but no child deserved to be unsafe, let alone in their own home by their father.

"Honestly, it's a blessing in disguise," Matthew continued. "I think he finally sees that our father has no interest in changing."

"Did he agree to go to school?"

"That's the plan." While Matthew softened during our embrace, there was still something off about the way he wouldn't look at me. I moved my head in an attempt to catch his eye.

"Matthew, look at me. What is going on?"

He exhaled before putting his large hands on my shoulders and stepping around me. Anxiety snaked up my arms and spread to my chest. He was pacing and refusing to look at me.

I pleaded with my eyes. *Please talk to me.*

"Lottie, we need to talk."

His words sounded hollow, and my stomach dropped. Goose bumps erupted on my arms as a million terrible thoughts raced through my mind.

When I didn't speak, he continued. "This"—his arms opened to gesture toward me—"has been incredible. *You* are incredible. Honestly, the best thing to ever happen to me."

I held tightly to the glimmer of hope that danced in my belly. I took one step forward, and, as he held his hand out, stopping me, the spark died.

"I hope you know that." He finally looked at me.

"But?" I asked, fighting the lump that had lodged in my throat.

"But . . . things are going to change. They *have* to change." He dragged a hand through his hair. "Kevin can start preparing for MSU. They have a transition program and a counselor that will get him started in a month or so."

The apartment was spinning. I had no idea what his brother's plans had to do with us, but I couldn't shake the sinking feeling that Matthew was about to shatter my heart.

"What does that have to do with us?"

"Look around, Lottie." He gestured to the small apartment. "This is it. This is all I have to offer you."

"I don't understand. There's nothing wrong with your home."

He scoffed at my words. "Stop. It's a shithole and you know it. Charlotte, you deserve so much more than I can give you."

I let his words sink in. While their meaning hurt, really, they pissed me off. "Matthew Bailey, how dare you?"

Surprise crossed his face.

I pointed a finger in his direction. "Yeah. How dare you. How dare you think that I want anything from you other than *you*." I gestured to all of him. "You are enough."

Matthew shook his head, nostrils flared. His body simmered with tension. "If I stay here, this is all I will ever be. It will never get any better than this."

I didn't understand what he was saying. "Stay here? Where are you going?"

Matthew walked toward the small dining room table and grabbed a slip of paper. He held it up to me. I took it, scanning the words, trying to make sense of what the hell was happening.

"After I sorted things out with Kevin, I knew. I knew I had to make a change if I could ever hope to be the kind of man that you deserve."

My eyes searched the paper for clarity.

I, Matthew Bailey . . .

. . . desiring to enlist in THE UNITED STATES MARINE CORPS *do declare that I was born, January 9 . . .*

"Matthew . . ." Tears flooded my eyes as awareness dawned on me. "Matthew, what did you do?"

He stood tall but swallowed hard. "Charlotte Perry, I'm in love with you, but I am not the man you deserve. I was fired from my job. When I needed to leave work again to help Kevin, my boss told me not to bother coming back. Said my family situation made me unreliable. If I stay here, I can't give you the things you're used to—the things you deserve."

My head swam, my heart sick, as his words flowed over me.

"Before I met you, I'd already been talking with a recruitment officer. I hesitated because I couldn't leave

Kevin. But now he'll be safe at school. He'll start a new life. I can send him the money I earn while I'm away."

"But the loan," I tried.

"Denied." His voice became flat.

"No. No, I approved the loan!" I stepped toward him and was met with coldness.

"Charlotte, I have the letter. It was denied."

It was impossible. I had approved his loan myself. I had to get to the bottom of it, but it was late, and I was still frantic over what Matthew was doing.

"How could you do this?" I was panicking, until shock was replaced by anger. "You claim to love me, but you do *this*? It doesn't make any sense."

His chest heaved. "This is my opportunity to make something of myself. To become more than the son of the town drunk. I leave for basic training at Camp Pendleton in California, and I'm not asking you to wait for me. I wouldn't do that to you. But I need you to know that there will never be anyone else. I think the Marines will suit me, and I'm hopeful it'll open doors for me that don't exist in Chikalu."

A riot of emotions raged inside me.

Confusion.

Anger.

Hurt.

"Charlotte"—he ran his hand gently from my shoulder to my elbow—"I will come back for you."

I calmed my features despite the war drum beating in my chest. I closed my eyes and took a deep breath before staring into his stupid, beautiful green eyes.

"Matthew, please don't take this the wrong way, but fuck you." He only blinked as I moved toward the door. "I'm happy that Kevin is safe. Enjoy your dinner. I expect my casserole dish to be returned."

With that, I walked out the door without looking back. My chin wobbled as I made my way to the car, refusing to let him see me break. Once I pulled onto the road, the dam broke, and tears poured out of me.

Instead of the much-anticipated date we'd planned, in the dim lighting of his apartment kitchen, Matthew Bailey had ripped my heart out.

TWELVE
MATTHEW

THE IMAGE of Charlotte's face, twisted with hurt as I told her the truth, had cut my heart out.

When she took a breath and leveled me with her eyes, it was chilling. She was furious, and sometimes the calm was scarier than the storm.

Holy shit, I fucked that up royally.

My eyes burned. I couldn't recall the last time I cried, but watching Charlotte nearly break down, fighting it as she walked toward her car, was brutal.

My apartment was too small. Stifling. I needed to escape. I threw open the back door and stomped down the stairs of the building. I mounted my bike and headed out of town.

Needing to burn up the rage bubbling inside me, I turned toward my friend Reed's house. He lived alone on a small piece of property, and when I'd lost my job at the garage, he'd agreed to let me park my Chevelle in his barn. I pulled up and took the spare key from my pocket.

In the dusty barn he'd converted into a garage, the Chevelle sat in all her purple glory. Maybe if I worked with my hands, the stab wound in my chest would ease a little. Not fifteen minutes into mindless tinkering, flashes of Charlotte flooded my mind. I couldn't escape her. Couldn't escape the wave of emotions that tormented me.

I slammed the wrench in my hand against my metal toolbox. Shock waves radiated up my arm and drowned out the voices in my head.

You're worthless.

I slammed the wrench into the toolbox again.

You'll never be what she deserves.

And again.

You made the wrong fucking choice.

And again.

A yell called out over the noise. "What the fuck, dude?"

My head whipped around, and I heaved as I fought to catch my breath. "Sorry, man."

"Seriously. What's going on?"

"Nothing." I threw the wrench into the dented toolbox and started cleaning up my space.

"Bullshit." My friend stood still, crossing his arms over his chest and waiting.

I tossed the last tool into the box and gave up. "I did it. I enlisted, like we'd talked about." When he didn't react, I kept going. "I know in my bones it's the right step for me. I need something different in my life. Something more than Chikalu Falls, man. But I met someone. She's everything. If I stay with her, I'll never be more than Lee Bailey's loser kid. If I leave, I'm leaving her."

Reed stood thoughtfully and nodded. "What did she have to say about you enlisting?"

My jaw clenched as shame rose inside me. "I knew I couldn't look her in the eye and still go through with it. So I finished the paperwork before I told her."

"That's fucked up."

I could see it in his eyes—he knew as well as I did that it was a mistake to not tell her.

"I know. But I know it's what's best. This gives me a career, some structure in my life. When I'm out, I'll come back. If she's still single, I'll fight like hell for a second chance. If she's not, I'll find a way to live with the knowledge that she found someone to make her happy." My gut burned thinking of Charlotte sharing her life with someone else. "She deserves more. I'm in love with her."

"Maybe. but you also didn't give her a choice. And that's not love."

His words hit me square in the chest as he turned to leave me in the dusty quiet of the garage.

"IF I HAD a girl like that, I sure as hell wouldn't be leaving her alone." Goddamn, the hits just kept coming. Once I made it back to my apartment, Kevin was out of the bedroom and waiting for me in the kitchen.

He hunched over the casserole Charlotte had left, eating it straight from the dish with a fork. I stomped toward the cabinet and yanked the door open. The small plate rattled in front of him as it wobbled and spun. He only shrugged and shoveled another forkful of food into his mouth.

I stared at the food. My gut churned. Everyone knew I'd fucked up, and there was nothing I could do about it. My fate was sealed. I would leave a very hurt and angry Charlotte behind. Rage poured through me.

It's an impossible choice.

There's nothing here I can offer her.

I'm doing my best.

Rather than eat, I resigned myself to my bedroom. As I lay on my bed, hands behind my throbbing head, I couldn't escape the thoughts of Charlotte. In the small amount of time I knew her, she'd changed everything for me—opened my eyes to possibilities I didn't even know existed.

I knew I would love her just as fiercely today as a lifetime from now, and I would be the man who deserved her love if it killed me.

THIRTEEN
CHARLOTTE

If I DIDN'T STAY busy, I would crumble. After leaving Matthew's house, I somehow made it back home without totaling my car and cried myself to sleep. For hours, sobs racked my body until I was so sick I could hardly move. The next morning I woke with puffy eyes, a raw throat, and a hole the size of Montana in my chest.

I called into work, claiming I had come down with the flu and spent a solid two days wallowing in bed. Every memory of Matthew was laced with the gut-wrenching reality of what he had done. I had fallen in love with him. He had said he loved me too.

How could he do this?

Anger still simmered below the pain of knowing Matthew was leaving for the Marines. It felt rash and sudden and unfair. Something had pushed him over the edge.

The loan.

Determined to get to the bottom of it, I forced myself to shower and dragged on something halfway decent before storming into the investment firm. All conversation stopped as I scanned the lobby. Unconcerned with the looks slanting my way, I moved toward the locked room that held our files and pulled out my keys.

"Charlotte, is everything okay?" Davis was concerned, and I barely spared him a glance as I growled and pushed through the door.

Unlocking the cabinet, I fingered through the files until I reached *Bailey, Matthew*. I gripped the file and pulled it from the cabinet. My fingers stalled when across the front page in angry red ink read *DENIED*.

"No. No!" I flipped through more pages, trying to understand what had happened, before coming across a copy of the letter sent to Matthew informing him that his application for a personal loan was denied.

"Charlotte, what is it?"

I held the paper toward Davis. "Why was this loan application altered? This file was approved by me personally!" I was spitting mad, and Davis was receiving the full brunt of my fury.

He grabbed the file from my hand but barely scanned it. *He knew*.

"Charlotte, darling." His tone dripped with condescension, and I wanted to punch him in the fucking face. "Your father entrusted me to help you here. He asked that I share with him any loans that you approved that may be . . . suspect."

"*Suspect?*" Forget punching him in the face. I was kneeing him in the balls if he took one step closer.

"Not in the best interest of the firm."

"How dare you? How fucking dare you! You went behind my back and changed the approval. It was *one* loan. Matthew was helping a kid afford school, you asshole!"

Davis looked around, horrified that my voice likely carried through the walls and into the lobby full of clients.

"Davis, you're fired." I crossed my arms in front of me and stood my ground.

He had the audacity to laugh. "You can't fire me."

Damn it. He's probably right.

I pointed one finger at him. "This isn't over."

Storming through the lobby, I didn't spare any of the customers a second glance. Still fuming, I clutched the papers as I yanked open my car door.

"What are you doing?" Trina's voice was laced with shock as she hustled up the sidewalk toward me. "I got a call that you raged through town, looking like you'd just survived a badger attack. What's up with you?"

"This!" I held the paper up.

She grabbed the paper from me and scanned it. "I don't get it."

"He sabotaged me. He was working behind the scenes with my father and made sure that Matthew's loan was denied." Tears welled as my voice got thick. "He was going to use that money to help Kevin in college!"

Trina's arms wrapped around me as I gave in to my meltdown.

"Surely it can be fixed. He can reapply and you can approve it this time."

I shook my head. "No. It's too late. When he got denied, he went and enlisted in the Marines. He's leaving, Trina."

"Oh that poor, stupid motherfucker." Trina's whisper was dripping with anger.

I wiped the tears and snot from my face, and she held me at arm's length. "You're a mess. Let's get you home and we'll figure this out." She moved me back and sat in the driver's seat. "Well?" She gestured toward the empty seat beside her.

"What about your car?"

"I can get it later. Let's get you home."

Having a girl like Trina in your corner was like winning the friendship lottery. She was strength and sunshine and made a fierce cup of coffee.

I held the warm mug between my hands and took a long sip.

"Careful, that one's got Irish cream liqueur in it."

I gave her a soft smile. "No wonder it tastes so good."

Trina sat across from me at my dining room table, resting her chin in her hand. "What are we gonna do with you?"

I closed my eyes and pressed my warm fingertips into my eyes and sighed. "I'm so . . . angry at him. But mostly? I'm heartsick."

"You have to remember, a guy like Matthew has lived his whole life in this town. Chikalu may be cute and quirky, but it's also *small*. Imagine trying to step out from the shadow of your entire family. Heck, even I thought Matthew Bailey was bad news. It wasn't until you gave him a chance that he had the courage to show a different side of himself."

"It was always there—the goodness. I love him, Trina."

"Sounds like there's only one thing to do."

I looked at my friend with hope as she continued. "You go get him." She shrugged as though it were the simplest thing in the world.

I nodded, stealing some of her confidence and letting

her words sink in. Matthew had lived his life feeling forgotten. Abandoned.

This just won't do.

I had no idea when Matthew was slated to leave for basic training, but I would never be able to live with myself if he left without knowing how I felt.

Yes, I was royally ticked off, but I could love him *and* be mad. My love for him meant that we could argue or fight, but all that meant was that we needed to go to our corners and figure our shit out.

Small towns had their benefits, as it was easy to keep tabs on him. I let him stew for a few days while Trina gave me ridiculously detailed updates on Matthew's day-to-day life. There were a few things that I needed to take care of at the office if my plan was really going to work.

Finally, when all the arrangements had been made and there was no going back, I walked up to his apartment and knocked on the heavy wood door.

When it opened, his brother, Kevin, smiled at me. He was smaller than Matthew and his hair much lighter, but they shared the same stormy green eyes. "Oh thank god," he said to me. "Matty! Someone's here," he called over his shoulder. "I'm going out!" Kevin eased past me and I just stared at him. "He's a wreck. Please don't break his heart."

Before I could reassure him, Kevin pushed his hands into his pockets and hurried away from the building. Matthew's large frame shadowed the doorway, and I craned my neck to look up at him. He hadn't shaved, the stubble adding a rugged sexiness to his scowl. His hair was disheveled, as though he'd dragged his hands through it one too many times. My body reacted to his warmth, pooling in my limbs.

When it registered that I was standing in his doorway, he paused.

I raised one hand. "Before you speak, I have something to say."

He looked down at me and nodded. A mixture of pain and longing had his eyes searching mine.

"You're an asshole. *But,*" I continued, "you're my asshole."

Matthew's voice was gravel as he spoke. "Lottie, I owe you an apology."

"Yes, you do. But I owe you one too. I am in love with you, Matthew Bailey. All parts of you. You're it for me." I let my hands slap the outsides of my thighs as I sighed. My chips were on the table. The ball in his court.

Matthew moved to hold my face in his hands. "I know I said before that I wouldn't ask you to wait, but I need to know. Lottie, will you wait for me?"

I steadied my breath before finally answering the most important question of our lives. "No."

FOURTEEN

MATTHEW

My HEART SANK into my boots, and I felt sick. Breathing was impossible.

This is it. I truly lost her.

"No, you idiot, I'm not waiting for you, because I'm coming with you."

My eyes flew to hers. She was smiling, her dark eyes radiant in the fading afternoon sunlight of my apartment. My mind raced as she continued. "I realized why you felt you needed to enlist. I also know that you're right—the Marines will give you something more that Chikalu can't. I know you'll serve your country with honor. But you also need to understand that I choose you. Every time. I will *always* choose you."

I could hardly get the words out, but I needed her to be sure. "What about your family? Their expectations and the life you're building here?"

She swatted a hand in the air like she wasn't making the most significant decision of our entire lives. "I'll deal with my family, and, sure, this town is growing on me, but I hate my job. Like, really, *really* hate it. I've already made arrangements for Davis to take over the office. If you're gone, all I'll do is feel hollow until you make your way back to me. I want to live my life. So let's do it. Let's move to California and have an adventure."

She was it for me.

This perfect, wild woman had stolen my heart and was offering me a second chance. One I probably didn't deserve. There's no way in hell I was letting her go again. I stepped toward her and held her hand before dropping to the ground.

"Marry me." Charlotte's dark eyes went wide. "Before you answer, I need you to know that I'm not asking you because I've enlisted. I knew from the second I saw you sitting on that bench in the corner of your yard that I would love you. If I thought there was even a chance you'd say yes, I would have asked you then. In my life I learned very early that needing someone only got you hurt. But I need you. There will never be another woman for me, Lottie. You're it for me. I will spend the rest of my life making you proud. I will always remember to show up for you and be the man you deserve."

Tears welled in her eyes, and she wiped one away before she gently cleared her throat. "There are some ground rules." I couldn't help but smile up at my girl. "If we're a team, then we make decisions together. I don't want to live my life worrying that you're going to try to fix something that we need to work on together. I need to trust that."

I stood, towering over her and holding both of her hands in mine. "Yes, ma'am. You have my word. What else?"

She squeezed my hand. "That's it. That's all I'll ever need from you." She stretched on her tiptoes and wrapped her arms around my neck. I breathed in her scent and squeezed around her middle. "Yes, Matthew Bailey. Yes! Yes! Yes!" I peppered kisses across her face as she continued, "Yes, yes, yes . . ."

Her laugh filled my soul.

EPILOGUE: MATTHEW

Four weeks after dropping to one knee and asking Lottie to marry me, Kevin was packed up and moving into a dorm at Montana State University. Charlotte had broken the news to her family. Her father yelled. Her mother cried. Her sister shot both fists into the air in triumph. Trina was her maid of honor as we said our vows in front of the justice of the peace.

I bought a suit from the secondhand store, and Lottie was gorgeous in a simple white dress. She chose wildflowers, and I picked them fresh just as I had for our very first date.

Then we sold what little belongings we had that couldn't come with us, including my bike. The rest was packed, and we headed west toward California in a Chevelle painted "plum crazy" purple. Lottie sang and cried and laughed as we made our way across the country.

I spent four hard years serving my country. When my time was up, we sat down and decided together that we were ready for a new adventure. Setting down roots brought us back to Chikalu Falls. Lottie's friend Trina had opened up a little clothing boutique and offered her a job. I'd spent my career as a tank mechanic, so finding work came easy.

Life was good.

"You ready for this?" I slapped a hand on the matte-black helmet on Charlotte's head. A riot of auburn hair peeked out from the sides as a huge grin split her face.

"Are you kidding me? I was born ready!" Lottie gripped the steering wheel of the muscle car I had been rebuilding.

"Okay, Hurricane. Remember, ten laps. Ease the corners and watch your blind spots. Hug the inside. Let the machine do the work."

My girl revved the engine, and it growled beneath her. "I'm gonna win."

I barked a laugh and leaned into the cab of the car to pull her sassy mouth to mine. "Don't drive wild. Stay focused."

The glint in her eye told me she was going to be reckless if it meant she was going to win the Powder Puff race. I only hoped she kept a cool head.

The announcer started talking, and I made my way back to the pit.

Seconds later the shot rang out and the sea of cars lurched forward. Lottie's black Impala stayed near the lead. Though she couldn't hear me, I shouted encouragement as she tore around the track. An impossibly fast car zoomed to take the lead. Lottie was hot on its tail. Lap after lap we cheered as the women fought to take the lead. They were racing for glory and honor. Bragging rights.

Lottie zipped past us but not before taking her eyes off the road for a second to shoot me a dazzling smile.

One lap to go.

I could tell by the way she drove she was confident.

When the checkered flag waved, pride filled my chest. My girl had done her best.

The racers rounded the track and one by one peeled off into their pits. Instead of making the turn, Charlotte simply waved her arms and screamed a *woo-hoo* as she drove right past us.

Oh fuck. Oh no.

Charlotte hadn't realized that back on lap three, she'd been passed. The winning car was more than half a lap in front of her, so the entire time she really thought she was winning.

As our entire pit crew waved our arms wildly, desperately trying to call her back into the pit, she continued to smile and wave and give us thumbs-up.

A friendly hand clamped down on my shoulder as I shook my head and laughed.

"Hell of a girl, that one."

"Yeah. Yeah she is."

When Charlotte finally completed her "victory lap," I could hardly contain the bubble of laughter as I broke the news to her.

She stared at me.

I thought she might cry until a howl of laughter erupted from her small body. "Stop it! No. No! But I . . . oh my god, that's the funniest thing I've ever heard."

Relieved, the entire crew laughed alongside her.

I threw my arm around her shoulders and pulled her close. "Come on, Number Two. Let's go home."

Lottie squirmed with the rumble of the motorcycle beneath her.

"Feels good, doesn't it?" Intent laced through my words.

"It's . . . been a while since we've ridden." She squirmed again.

I cupped the back of her knee, hitching her leg closer to me and leaning back so she could hear me. "Once you come on the back of a bike, you'll never want to drive a car again. Hold on and enjoy the ride."

By the time we reached the county line, she was primed and ready to go. The adrenaline from the race had been replaced by all-consuming lust. When I pulled down an unfamiliar road, her grip around me tightened.

A copse of trees hid my surprise as I slowed down the gravel path. Finally, we rounded a corner and a large white farmhouse came into view. I pulled up to the house, emotion stretching open my chest.

I cut the engine and stared at it.

"Matthew, where are we?"

I cupped behind her knee again and leaned into her. "Home."

Her eyes went wide.

"I know I promised that all big decisions would be team decisions, so technically it's not home yet. But if you want it, it's yours."

Her mouth dropped open. The large home had shiny black shutters and a massive wrap-around porch. It sat in a large clearing overlooking the river. A few small outbuildings dotted the property, and I could see our whole lives unfolding in front of us.

"I was thinking we'd stop renting. Put down some roots. Make a new name for the Baileys in Chikalu Falls." I had never outrun my past, and a few in town still gave me a wide berth when I walked down the sidewalk, but I was finding my way. When my father died, Lottie and I were the only ones at the funeral. She held my hand as I let myself let him go.

"Matthew Lee Bailey!" She squealed in delight as she dismounted the motorcycle and ran toward the house. She turned a wide circle, her arms spread out. "Yes!" she shouted.

I ran to her, scooping her into my arms.

She rained kisses down my face as I held her tightly. Quickly, our mouths went from playful to passionate as I pulled her into me.

Hot and greedy, I hauled her over my shoulder as I stomped up the steps of the house. With a smack on her ass, I caressed the back of her thighs.

Setting her on the top step, I spread her knees wide and squatted in front of her. "What do you say?"

Her arms looped around my neck and pulled her mouth to my ear. "You had better fuck me on the porch of our new home."

Surging forward, I laid Charlotte down as I covered her body with mine. Frantic kisses turned slow and languid as I savored my woman. Charlotte Bailey was every one of my fantasies come to life. I reached behind me to pull my shirt off.

Lottie's hand came up to toy with the small chain that hung around my neck. "I love that you still wear this."

"Next to you, it's my most precious thing."

When she moaned into our kiss, my cock thickened beneath the zipper of my jeans. If she wanted me to take her out in the open, right on the porch that would become our home, I would.

My hands moved over her rib cage to her breasts, reveling in the comfort and familiarity of her figure. Her nipples were taut, and I plucked one between my fingers.

Our years together ensured I knew exactly what she liked, but I was always searching for new ways to pleasure her.

I made quick work of removing her pants and underwear, leaving her top in place. It was unlikely anyone would venture this far out of town and discover us, but with her I wouldn't take any chances. I pulled my cock from my jeans and gave it a long, hard tug.

My fingers slid through her folds, swirling her wet heat against her clit.

"You don't need the special moves. I want quick and dirty."

Quick and dirty.

I preferred to take my time with Lottie, but the heat pumping out of her told me she was primed and ready. I stretched her pussy with my fingers before clamping my mouth onto the pulse point in her neck and spearing her hard with my cock.

She was slick and I fit right in. She pulsed around me as she cried out. My hand moved over her lips. "Shh. Don't wake the neighbors," I teased.

She panted as I pumped into her. "There are no neighbors."

I bit at the thin skin in her neck. "I know. That was part of the appeal."

My back tightened, my cock and balls aching to feel her pulse around me.

"I want this house, Matthew. I want it with you."

"Yes, baby. It's yours. I promise to give you everything you want."

I kissed her long and deep as she came around my cock. My dick twitched and balls pulled in tight as I surrendered to my release.

Wrapped in her, I breathed her in, as I always did.

Despite the years that were passing, I still couldn't get enough of this incredible woman.

I still didn't deserve her, but I'd be damned if I didn't try every single day.

Charlotte was a woman who showed up for you. When you were down on your luck, desperate for a change, she showed me that I was worth showing up for.

I may not have had much of a choice. From the moment we met, I was a goner. But despite the odds, she chose me right back.

IF YOU ENJOYED READING Matthew and Charlotte's love story, please consider leaving a review—they make a huge difference for indie authors!

SNEAK PEEK OF FINDING YOU

CHIKALU FALLS BOOK 1

Lincoln

Three Years Ago

The jolt from the blast rattled through the truck, blowing out the front window. All of the doors flew open. Unlatched, I was ejected from the vehicle—thrown onto the open road. I slid before coming to a grunting halt against a nearby building.

I remember every second of it. There's no way to describe how it feels when you think you're going to die. No white light, no moment of clarity. The one thing that crossed my mind was that I wanted to kill the motherfuckers who did this.

With so much adrenaline pumping through my veins, I couldn't feel a thing. The blast from the IED into the truck as we were leaving a neighboring village also meant that I couldn't hear shit. I knew from his anguished face Duke was screaming, writhing on the ground, but as I stared at him, I heard nothing but a low ringing between my ears.

Smoke swirled around me as I fought to get my bearings. My eyes felt like they were lined with sandpaper, and my lungs couldn't seem to drag in enough air.

Get up. You're a sitting duck. Get. The fuck. UP.

Dragging myself to my knees, I patted down my most tender places, and except for my right arm, which hurt like a bitch, I was fine. I looked back at Duke, whose face had gone still. Although I already knew, I checked his vitals, but it was pointless. Fanned out around us were eight or nine other casualties—some Americans, some villagers. One set of little feet in sandals I just couldn't look at.

Ducking behind another car, I drew my gun and swept the crowd. *Come on, motherfucker, show yourself.* Civilians were getting up, walking past like nothing had happened. Those affected by the blast were screaming, begging. It was a total clusterfuck. My eyes darted around the area, but I couldn't find the trigger man. He'd melted into the crowd.

I ran back toward the mangled, smoking remains of our Humvee. Fuck. It was a twisted mess of metal and blood. Crouching around the base of the truck, I moved to find the guys. Lying in the dirt, knocked halfway out of the doorframe, was Keith, hanging on by the cables of the radio, his left leg torn at a sickening angle. He was dazed, staring at the pooling blood staining the dirt around him and growing at an alarming rate. Without my med kit, I had to improvise. I ripped his belt from his waist and using that and a piece of metal, successfully made the world's worst tourniquet around his upper thigh.

Over the constant, shrill ringing in my ears, I yelled at him, "I got you! FOCUS. Look at me . . . We got this!"

His nod was weak, and his color pallid. He probably only had minutes, and that was not going to fucking happen. I grabbed the radio mic. The crackle of the speaker let me know we weren't totally fucked. Calling in a bird was the only way we were getting out of this shithole.

"This is Corpsman Lincoln Scott. Medevac needed. Multiple down."

"10-4. This is Chop-4. Extent of injuries."

"We've got a couple hit here. Ah, fuck, Wade took two in the chest. At least four down."

"Roger that. Let's get you men onboard."

Leaning back on the truck, weapon across my legs, I felt warmth spread across my neck and chest. The adrenaline was wearing off, and I became aware of the pain in my neck, shooting down my ribs and arm, vibrating through my skull. Reaching up with my left arm, I traced my fingertips along my neckline and felt my shirt stick to my skin. Moving back, I found a hot, hard lump of metal protruding from my shoulder and neck. It had buddies too—shrapnel littering my upper torso, arm, and neck. My fingers grazed the pocket of my uniform, and I held my hand there. I could feel the outline of the letter I kept in my pocket. Its presence vibrated through me. Touching my right forearm, I thought about my tattoo beneath the uniform. Looking down, all I could see were shreds of my uniform and thick, red blood.

Hold steady. Breathe.

My fingers explored. My vest was the only thing that kept the worst of the blast from reaching my vital organs. This neck wound though . . . damn. This wasn't great.

The cold prick of panic crept up my legs and into my chest.

Calm the fuck down. Stop dumping blood because you can't keep your shit together. Breathe.

I focused on Keith's shallow, staccato breathing next to me. I tried to turn my head, but that wasn't fucking happening. "You good, man?"

"Shit, doc. Never better."

"Hah. Atta boy."

We sat in labored-breathing silence. Listened for the medevac helicopters. As the scene around us came into focus, I realized how easily the lifeless bodies of the Marines around me could have been mine. I counted six members of my platoon killed or badly wounded. Our machine gun team, Mendez and Tex, had been among the dead. Mendez was only twenty.

Already struggling to breathe, I felt the wind knock out of me. Just last week, in a quiet moment outside our tent, Mendez told me he was afraid. He missed his mom and little sister and just wanted to go home to Chicago. Becoming a Marine was a mistake, he'd said.

"Doc, I don't wanna die out here, man."

In that quiet moment, he'd revealed what we all felt, but never spoke aloud. Instead of offering him some comfort, I'd stared out into the blackness of the desert by his side until he turned, stubbed out his cigarette, and walked back inside.

Leaning my head back, I let my own thoughts wander to Finn and Mom. His easy smile, her lilting laugh. I wondered what they were doing back home while I was slowly dying, an imposter in the desert.

When I walked off the plane, the airport had an eerie feeling of calm. I could smell the familiar summer Montana air over the lingering stale bagels and sweat of the airport. I hoisted my rucksack over my shoulder and began to walk toward the exit when a small voice floated over my right shoulder. "Thank you for your service."

My whole body shifted, I still couldn't turn my head quite right, and I peered down at a little boy—probably six or seven at most. "Hey, little man. You're welcome."

Then he clipped his heels together and saluted, and I thought I'd die right there. He was so fucking cute. I saluted back to him and dropped to my knee.

"You know, they give these to us because we're strong and brave and love our country." I peeled the American flag patch off my shoulder, felt its soft Velcro backing run through my fingers. "I think you should have it."

The little boy's eyes went wide, and his mother put her hand over her heart, teared up, and mouthed, "Thank you." I tipped my head to her as I stood.

"Linc! LINCOLN!" I heard Finn yell above the crowd and turned to see my younger brother running through baggage claim. His body slammed into me, and we held onto each other for a moment. I ignored the electric pain sizzling down my arm. Over his shoulder, I could see Mom, tears in her eyes, running with a sign.

"Damn, kid. We missed you!" Finn laughed, his sprawling hand connecting with my shoulder. I braced myself, refusing to wince at his touch. But Finn was huge, a solid two inches taller than my six-foot-one-inches. He'd definitely grown up, reminding me that he wasn't the same gap-toothed fifteen-year-old kid I'd left behind when I enlisted.

"Kid? Don't forget I'm older and can still beat the shit out of you. Hey, Mom." I engulfed my mother in a hug. Her tiny frame reminded me why everyone called her Birdie.

"Eight years. Almost a decade and now I get to keep you forever!" We hugged again, her thin arms holding onto me tighter, nails digging into my uniform. Mom was a crier. If we didn't get this under control now, we'd be here all afternoon with her trying to fuss all over me like I was eleven and just wrecked my dirt bike. But the truth was, while I'd been home for the occasional holiday leave, Chikalu Falls, Montana hadn't been my home for over a decade.

She finally released the hug, holding me at arm's length. "I'm so happy to have you home," she sighed.

"I'm happy too, Mom." It was only a small lie, but I had to give it to her. I was happy to see her and Finn, and to put the death and dirt and sand behind me. But I'd planned on at least another tour in the Marines. I was almost through my second enlistment when the IED explosion tore through my body. The punctured lung, torn flesh, and scars were the easy part. It was the nerve damage to my right arm and neck that was the real problem.

Unreliable trigger finger wasn't something the United States Marine Corps wanted in their ranks. In the end, after the doctors couldn't get my neck to turn or the pain radiating down my right arm to settle, I'd been honorably discharged.

I glanced down at the poster board that Finn scooped off the ground. "Oh, Great. You Somehow Survived" was written in bubble letters with a haphazard smattering of sequins and glitter. Laughing, I adjusted my pack and looked at Finn. "You're such a dick." I had to mumble it under my breath to make sure Mom didn't hear me, but from the corner of my eye, I could see her smirk.

"Let's go, boys."

It was a four-hour trip from Spokane, Washington to

Chikalu Falls, Montana—but only out-of-towners used its full, given name. Saying Chikalu was one way to tell the locals from the tourists.

The drive was filled with Mom's updates on day-to-day life in our small hometown. Finn eagerly filled me in on his fishing guide business, how he wanted to expand, and how I could help him run it. I listened, occasionally grunting or nodding in agreement as I stared out the window at the passing pines. Ranches and farmland dotted the landscape as we weaved through the national forest.

I was going home.

"You know, Mr. Bailey's been asking about you. He heard you were coming home and wants to make sure that you stop in...when you're settled," Mom said.

"Of course. I always liked Mr. Bailey. I'm glad to hear he's still kicking."

Finn laughed. "Still kicking? That old man's never gonna die. He's still sitting out in his creepy old farmhouse, complaining about all the college kids and how they're ruining all the fishing. I saw him walk into town with a rifle on his shoulder last week like that's not completely against the law. People straight up scatter when he walks through town. It's amazing."

Changing the subject, Mom glanced at me over her shoulder and chimed in with, "The ladies at the Chikalu Women's Club are all in a flutter, what with you coming home this week. You make five of our seven boys who've come home now." A heavy silence blanketed the car as her words floated into the air. No one acknowledged that three of the five who'd returned came home in caskets.

Clearing her throat gently, she added, "And you got everyone's letters?"

I nodded. The Chikalu Women's Club was known around my platoon for their care packages and letters. Without fail, every birthday, holiday, and sometimes "just because," I would get a small package. Sometimes because we'd moved around or simply because the mail carrier system was total shit, the packages would be weeks or months late, but inside were drawings from school kids, treats, toiletries, and letters. I'd share the candies and toiletries with the guys. We'd barter over the Girl Scout cookies. A single box of Samoas was worth its weight in gold. For me, the letters became the most important part. Mostly they were from Mom and Finn, young kids or other mothers, college students working on a project, that kind of thing.

But in one package in November, I got the letter that saved my life.

I idly touched the letter in my shirt pocket. Six years. For six years, I'd carried that letter with me. After the bombing, it was torn and stained with my blood, and you could hardly read it now, but it was with me.

"The packages were great. They really helped to boost morale around camp. I tried writing back to the kids who wrote when I could. Some of them didn't leave a return address," I said.

Mom continued filling the space with anecdotes about life around Chikalu. My thoughts drifted to the first time I'd opened the package and saw the letter that saved me.

In that package, there had been plenty of treats—trail mix, gum, cookies, beef jerky, cheese and cracker sandwiches. When you're in hell, you forget how much you miss something as simple as a cheese and cracker sandwich. Under the treats was a neat stack of envelopes. Most were addressed to "Marine" or "Soldier" or "Our Hero" and a few were addressed directly to me. I always got one from Mom and Finn. When I got the packages, I shared some of the letters with the guys in camp. The ones marked "Soldier" were always given to the grunt we were giving shit to that week. Soldiers were in the Army, but we were Marines.

On the bottom of this particular box was a thick, doodled envelope—colored swirls and shapes covering the entire outside. It was addressed directly to me in swirly feminine handwriting. Turning it over in my hands, I felt unsettled. An uncomfortable twinge in my chest had me rattled. I didn't like not feeling in control, so rather than opening it right away, I stored it in my footlocker.

I couldn't shake the feeling that the letter was calling to me. I spent three days obsessing over the doodles on the envelope—was it an art student from the college? The mystery of it was intoxicating. Why was it addressed to me if I had no idea who had written it? When I finally opened it, I was spellbound. The letter wasn't written like a traditional letter where someone was anonymously writing notes of encouragement or thanks. This letter was haphazard. Different inks, some cursive, some print, quotes on the margins.

It became clear that the letter had been written over the course of several days. The author had heard about the town letter collection and decided to write to me on a whim. It included musings about life in a small mountain town, tidbits of information learned in a college class, facts about the American West, even a knock-knock joke about desert and dessert. I read that letter every day until a new one came. Similarly decorated envelope, same nonlinear ramblings inside. A voice—her voice—came through in those letters.

There were moments in the dark I could imagine her

laughter or imagine feeling her breath on my ear as she whisper-sang the lyrics she'd written. Her letters brought me comfort in those dark moments when I doubted I'd ever have my mom's buttermilk pie again or hear Finn laugh at a really good joke.

Over the years, she included small pieces of information about who she was. Not anyone I'd known pre-enlistment, but a transplant from Bozeman. She'd gone to college in Chikalu. "The mountains and the river are my home," she wrote. Her letters were funny, charming, comforting.

The one I carried with me was special. News reports of conflict in the Middle East were everywhere, and she'd assumed correctly that I was right in the thick of it. She told me the story of the Valkyrie she'd learned about in one of her courses.

In Norse mythology, Valkyrie were female goddesses who spread their wings and flew over the battlefield, choosing who lived and who died in battle. Warriors chosen by the Valkyrie died with honor and were then taken to the hall of Valhalla in the afterlife. Their souls could finally rest.

Reading her words, I felt comfort knowing that if I held my head high and fought with honor, she would come for me. I carried her words in my head. Through routine sweeps or high-intensity missions, her words would wash over me, motivate me, and steady me. She connected with something inside of my soul—deep and unfamiliar. At my next leave, I'd gotten a tattoo of the Valkyrie wings spread across my right forearm so I could have a visual reminder of her. I could always keep her with me.

Glancing down now, I slid my sleeve up, revealing the bottom edge of the tattoo. It was marred with fresh, angry scars but it was there. My goddess had been with me in battle, and I'd survived.

Pulling into town, I knew I had to find her—the woman who left every letter signed simply: *Joanna.*

Continue reading Finding You

ACKNOWLEDGMENTS

First and foremost, I have to thank my parents for having the cutest meet-cute to ever exist. I grew up asking them over and over to retell the story of my mom waiting outside her friend's house when my dad drove by on his motorcycle, saw her, and turned his bike around. He was the older bad boy with a reputation and she was the sweet, new girl in town. To this day he can still recall exactly what she wore and exactly how he felt. ***Swoon.*** The rest is total fiction (at least that's what I'm telling myself).

To Jake—you're always an amazing partner, husband, and father. I could never have "snuck a novella" into my writing schedule without your encouragement, support, and ability to pick up the slack when I'm freaking out about deadlines. Every love story I write is inspired, in microscopic ways, by the love you bring to my life.

Leanne—don't ever leave me. I will find you. Not only are you an amazing hype woman, but you created a fabulous design that gave Old Man Bailey a smokin' hot cover. Who knew that grump could look so good? I am so thankful to have you in my corner, cheering me on and always being available to bounce ideas off of. I think I just ended that sentence incorrectly, but because you love me, you won't call me out on it. Probably. #dreamteam

Big thanks to my gorgeous work wife, Elsie. Our daily check ins are a highlight of my day. Had it not been for our highly productive sprint sessions, this novella would likely not exists. I trust you in all things and one of these days, I'm going to be in the same time zone to tell you that over a gigantic glass of wine. 3, 2, 1, duck.

To Morgan James for asking me to be a part of the Bad Boys of Summer anthology—without that push, I wouldn't have carved out the time to bring Matthew Bailey's story to life. Your organizational skills are unrivaled and it was a pleasure creating with you!

Vixens!! Thank you for being an incredible street team. You always know how to make a girl feel good and share my dirty stories with the world. I wouldn't be where I am today without your support and sharing on social media.

To each and every reader who comes with me on this incredible journey—I am so thrilled you're as excited as I am to return to Chikalu Falls! From my debut novel, Finding You, I knew Old Man Bailey deserved his own HEA. I hope you love it as much as I do!

ABOUT THE AUTHOR

Lena Hendrix is a contemporary romance author living in the Midwest. Her love for romance stared with sneaking racy Harlequin paperbacks and now she writes her own hot-as-sin small town romance novels. Lena has a soft spot for strong alphas with marshmallow insides, heroines who clap back, and sizzling tension. Her novels pack in small town heart with a whole lotta heat.

When she's not writing or devouring new novels, you can find her hiking, camping, fishing, and sipping a spicy margarita!

Want to hang out? Find Lena on Tiktok or IG!

Printed in Great Britain
by Amazon

25907962R00078